MW01702833

THE WORLD'S
WORST CONCEPT CARS

THE WORLD'S WORST CONCEPT CARS

FROM CREATIVE FAILURES TO BREATHTAKINGLY UGLY DISASTERS

RICHARD DREDGE

METRO BOOKS
NEW YORK

© 2010 by Amber Books Ltd

This 2010 edition published by Metro Books,
by arrangement with Amber Books Ltd.

All rights reserved. No part of this publication may be reproduced, stored in a retrieval system, or transmitted, in any form or by any means, electronic, mechanical, photocopying, recording, or otherwise, without prior written permission from the publisher.

Editorial and design by
Amber Books Ltd

Project Editor: James Bennett
Picture Research: Terry Forshaw
Design: Colin Fielder

All images courtesy of magiccarpics.co.uk

Metro Books
122 Fifth Avenue
New York, NY 10011

ISBN: 978-1-4351-2266-6

Printed and bound in Thailand

M 10 9 8 7 6 5 4 3 2 1

CONTENTS

INTRODUCTION

The future has always held a fascination for us, because we want to get a glimpse of it before it arrives. Concept cars often give us the opportunity to look into the future – but often those who forecast what's on the way are seriously detached from reality, as illustrated all too well within these pages.

Above: *Rinspeed has probably produced more pointless concepts than anybody – but the X Dream, as shown here, was unfeasibly ugly into the bargain.*

While the car has developed at a relatively slow rate since the first machines trundled out of sheds in the 1880s, in the minds of far-sighted designers, automobiles have forever been on the brink of turning into something which can glide above the ground, usually driving itself while using

Above: *The Moovie was Peugeot's take on a city car of the future; it was perfect for anybody who wanted to be a laughing stock on the streets.*

a minimum of resources in the process. Other common themes include aircraft-style aerodynamics, jaw-dropping technology and phenomenal efficiency.

Sadly, the reality has rarely lived up to the hype. More than a century after the car arrived, there's still no auto-pilot, cars still need a road on which to drive, and in most cases use the same basic mechanical layout that was adopted a dozen or so decades ago. As a result of this overreaching ambition, over the next five chapters we'll take a look at some of the far-sighted cars that never stood a chance, those that offered nothing of any use to anyone, as well as those which simply shouldn't have got as far as the drawing board, never mind a running prototype.

CHAPTER 1: BAD DESIGN

If the point of a concept car is to test reaction, it's best to come up with something that isn't so unattractive that it will frighten children or alarm pedestrians. All of the cars in this chapter were wilfully ugly or – even worse – they took an existing car that was at worst inoffensive, and turned it into a four-wheeled horror.

In the latter category was Bertone's 308GT Rainbow, which butchered one of the most beautiful cars of the time (Ferrari's 308GTB) to turn it into something so nasty that when the car was offered for sale, not a single person put their hands into their pockets. From the hideously disjointed Italdesign Columbus to the bloated Lincoln Machete, taking in the ridiculously proportioned Russo Baltique Impression along the way, all the concepts here featured designs which were nothing less than a complete disaster. Indeed, the cars in this chapter were so badly proportioned, awkwardly styled or just plain ugly that none of the themes they previewed ever stood any hope of reaching production in any form – which made them rather pointless as glimpses of the future.

Left: The Russo Baltique Impression revived a badge that had died decades before. They shouldn't have bothered...

BEECHCRAFT PLAINSMAN (1946)

Business remained buoyant for Beech Aircraft Corporation throughout World War II, with plenty of orders being placed for its aircraft. But when war turned to peace things looked bleak; suddenly the order book looked a bit thin, and an alternative plan was needed to keep the company thriving. Beech decided that its future lay in car manufacture, so it hurriedly knocked up a prototype, which it called the Plainsman. Packed full of safety and comfort features, the car may have been far-sighted, but it was also ugly and impractical. In the end the car was not needed; the US government placed orders for millions of dollars worth of military aircraft soon after the war's end, assuring Beech's future and allowing it quietly to forget about any forays into car production.

SPECIFICATION

ORIGIN	USA
DEBUT	1946
ENGINE CAPACITY	N/A
CONFIGURATION	Rear-mounted
TRANSMISSION	Rear-wheel drive
POWER	N/A
TOP SPEED	257km/h (160mph)
LENGTH	N/A
WIDTH	N/A

Left: *The Plainsman had adjustable air suspension all round, which automatically calibrated itself according to the load and weight distribution.*

Safety featured heavily, with rubber crash pads around the cabin and solenoid-activated doors that meant protruding internal handles could be dispensed with.

Visibility was very important, which is why the glasshouse was so deep. There were also auxiliary panes along the edge of the car's roof.

The prototype featured an engine mounted in the rear, but production cars could accommodate an engine in the front instead, if necessary.

Looking big and very heavy, the Plainsman resembled the Czechoslovakian Tatra, thanks mainly to that very bulky rear end treatment.

BERTONE 308 GT RAINBOW (1976)

If you were asked to name all the Ferraris that have not been drop-dead gorgeous, you would have to resort to special-bodied cars and the 308 GT4. The latter is the only production Ferrari designed by Bertone (all the rest have been Pininfarina confections), which just goes to prove one thing: Bertone should stay away from the prancing horse. But having made a complete hash of creating a four-seater Ferrari, Bertone could not resist trying to improve the 308 GTB – coming up with this. Bizarrely, the car was offered at $200,000 in the 1978 Marshall Fields Christmas catalogue – but with an 18-month wait, it does not seem that anybody gave into temptation. If there was any.

SPECIFICATION

ORIGIN	Italy
DEBUT	1976
ENGINE CAPACITY	2927cc (179cu in)
CONFIGURATION	Mid-mounted V8
TRANSMISSION	Five-speed manual, rear-wheel drive
POWER	190kW (255bhp)
TOP SPEED	254km/h (158mph)
LENGTH	4310mm (170in)
WIDTH	1860mm (73in)

Left: *The Rainbow tag came from the 308's ability to cope with rain or shine. This was hardly a unique feature, as it applied to pretty much any production car being made then.*

Ferrari's 308 GTB donated its 3-litre V8, mounted behind the two occupants, driving the rear wheels via a five-speed gearbox.

Where the donor car, the Ferrari 308 GTB, was a mass of curves, the Rainbow was all straight lines and angles. Some called it distinctive – 'eyesore' summed it up better.

Instead of a folding cloth roof, there was a fixed panel above the occupants that rotated around its rearward edge, before sliding behind the seats where it was stowed when not in use.

Nearly 10cm (four inches) was cut out of the wheelbase; the Rainbow also sat more than 12.5cm (five inches) lower than the 308 GT4.

BERTONE SUAGNA (2007)

The problem with coupé-cabriolets is making them look good when the roof is up. They are invariably OK when the roof is stowed, but the measure of any successful coupé-cabriolet design is its visual appeal with the roof raised. The Bertone Suagna is proof of this; in top-down mode it is inoffensive, but stick that roof up and suddenly the thing is hideous, primarily because of a disjointed rear end that should never have been signed off. Still, with a back catalogue as extensive as Bertone's, you cannot expect them to get it spot on every time. Somewhere close would have been nice …

SPECIFICATION

ORIGIN	Italy
DEBUT	Geneva 2007
ENGINE CAPACITY	N/A
CONFIGURATION	Front-mounted four-cylinder
TRANSMISSION	Front-wheel drive
POWER	N/A
TOP SPEED	N/A
LENGTH	4173mm (164in)
WIDTH	1773mm (70in)

Left: *The Suagna took its name from a Piedmontese word meaning 'a job done painstakingly'. Clearly not painstakingly enough in this case.*

As is typical with a coupé-cabriolet, the rear deck was too high to sit comfortably with the rest of the car's lines.

A key feature was the unusually small back window, which could be retracted separately from the roof to allow for fresh air in the rain.

Thanks to Bertone's long-standing relationship with Fiat, the Suagna was based on a Grande Punto; which derivative was not disclosed.

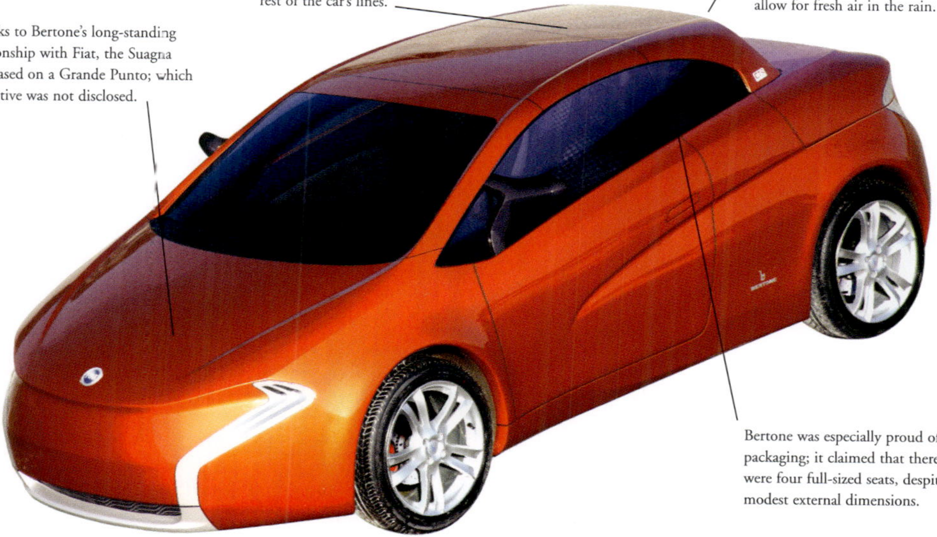

Bertone was especially proud of the packaging; it claimed that there were four full-sized seats, despite the modest external dimensions.

BMW XCOUPÉ (2001)

Nobody could have foreseen the full horror of what would emerge from BMW's styling studios in the years after the arrival of the xCoupé. Here was a car that previewed Chris Bangle's flame surfacing – a school of design that complicated panelwork beyond comprehension, looking as uncoordinated as possible. While it's true that elements of flame surfacing would look good and other car manufacturers would also use it (sparingly), that didn't prevent the xCoupé from looking like a complete dog's breakfast, with its nasty lack of symmetry. Years after its unveiling its shock value has reduced, but it is still no shining example of automotive good looks.

SPECIFICATION

ORIGIN	Germany
DEBUT	Detroit 2001
ENGINE CAPACITY	2926cc (179cu in), turbocharged
CONFIGURATION	Front-mounted straight-six diesel
TRANSMISSION	Five-speed auto, four-wheel drive
POWER	137kW (184bhp)
TOP SPEED	200km/h (125mph)
LENGTH	4580mm (180in)
WIDTH	1869mm (74in)

Left: *Four-wheel drive and a 3-litre (179cu in) straight-six diesel engine were borrowed from BMW's X5 to give the xCoupé strong performance with fuel economy.*

Although the xCoupé did not see production, the Z4 used the same aggressive nose treatment and 'flame surfacing' design language.

The asymmetrical lines of the xCoupé are not immediately apparent from every angle – but in the metal it was hugely controversial.

The headlights swivelled with the front wheels to light the car's way, via a link to the steering system, controlled by GPS.

The xCoupé's alloy wheels were 50cm (20in) in diameter, and no spare wheel was needed because the tyres had run-flat technology.

BMW Z18 (2000)

To be fair to BMW, the Z18 was never introduced as a showgoing concept as such. It was a test-bed for future technologies and therefore did not require sleek styling – but BMW clearly felt that it would impress a few people, which is why the company released official images of it. Even BMW must have realized that the Z18 was no looker, though, because it never showed the car officially – indeed, there is no record of the car ever having gone on public display. And that is an illustration of just how ugly this car was. While many of BMW's models have been pretty appalling, this was just too much, even for BMW.

SPECIFICATION

ORIGIN	Germany
DEBUT	2000
ENGINE CAPACITY	4398cc (268cu in)
CONFIGURATION	Front-mounted V8
TRANSMISSION	Manual, four-wheel drive
POWER	213kW (286bhp)
TOP SPEED	N/A
LENGTH	N/A
WIDTH	N/A

Left: *Inside the Z18 there was space for just two people, and the car's very simply laid-out cabin would go on to heavily influence that of the Z8 roadster.*

BMW started working on the Z18 in 1995; you'd think the company could come up with something far more appealing after five years.

The mechanicals were pure X5, which meant a four-wheel drive transmission with motive power from a 4.4-litre (268cu in) V8.

This was a cross between an SUV and a roadster, which is why there was so much ground clearance – and why it looked so odd.

To keep weight down, the bodyshell was made of plastic. Oddest styling feature was the cycle wing (fender) underneath the conventional wings.

BMW Z22 (2000)

In the same way that the Z18 was never displayed officially at any motor show, the Z22 was also a test-bed that was unveiled to the world through the press only. A very different kind of car from the Z18 roadster, the Z22 was all about carrying a family of five as efficiently as possible – and that's certainly an admirable goal. It does not matter how space-efficient a car is, though, if it looks like a complete mishmash, nobody is going to buy it. This must have been why BMW did not use any of the styling themes featured in the Z22 in any of its production cars.

SPECIFICATION

ORIGIN	Germany
DEBUT	2000
ENGINE CAPACITY	2 litres (122cu in)
CONFIGURATION	Mid-mounted four-cylinder
TRANSMISSION	CVT, rear-wheel drive
POWER	101kW (136bhp)
TOP SPEED	N/A
LENGTH	N/A
WIDTH	N/A

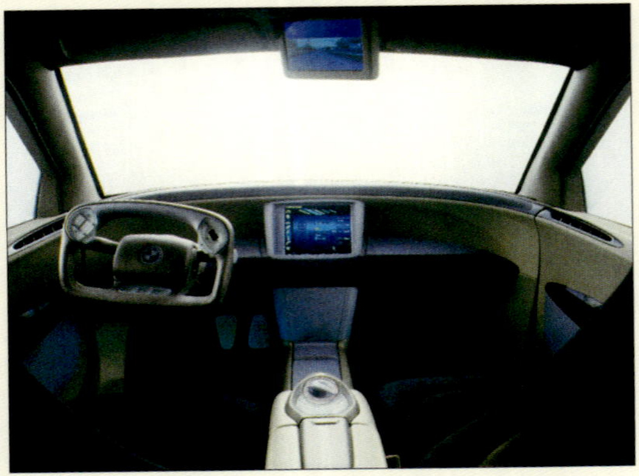

Left: *Despite being let down on the design front, the Z22 was most definitely a cutting-edge concept. It featured 70 innovations, and BMW applied for 61 patents with it.*

The Z22 was the same length as a 3-Series, yet it featured a wheelbase the same as that on a 7-Series – hence the odd proportions.

The bodyshell weighed about half that of a regular production car, thanks to the aluminium frame and carbon-fibre/alloy panelling.

Other weight-saving measures included titanium suspension springs, magnesium alloy wheels and carbon-fibre brake discs.

There was no mechanical linkage in the steering; instead it was drive-by-wire, with a variable ratio of between 0.8 and 3.0 turns between locks.

BUGATTI EB112 *(1993)*

If you are spending zillions on anything, you expect it to look great and work amazingly. When it is a car, the former is especially important – after all, you don't want people looking at you for all the wrong reasons, do you? Where the EB112 was concerned, this was a distinct possibility, courtesy of a design that jarred from every angle. Up front was a grille that worked fine on Bugatti's pre-war cars, but here it was contrived. The rear view was no better; it was bulbous and nondescript. The real tragedy was that this was a design from Giorgetto Giugiaro, an automotive design genius. Still, it just goes to show that even design geniuses can have off days.

SPECIFICATION

ORIGIN	Italy
DEBUT	Geneva 1993
ENGINE CAPACITY	5995cc (366cu in)
CONFIGURATION	Front-mounted V12
TRANSMISSION	Six-speed manual, four-wheel drive
POWER	339kW (455bhp)
TOP SPEED	300km/h (186mph)
LENGTH	5090mm (200in)
WIDTH	1990mm (78in)

Left: *The EB112's interior was all you would expect of a costly luxury car. It was crammed with standard equipment and clothed in expensive materials.*

Bugatti set out to break the 300km/h (186mph) barrier with the B112, thanks to a 339kW (455bhp) V12 powerplant.

The car was designed as the world's fastest four-door saloon (sedan); at that time the 285km/h (177mph) Lotus Carlton beat all comers.

To maximize the EB112's top speed, weight was kept to a minimum through the use of a carbon-fibre chassis and aluminium body panels.

Also aiding the car's performance was an incredibly slippery bodyshell, with flush glass and plenty of swooping curves.

BUICK SIGNIA *(1998)*

Beaten big time with the ugly stick, the Signia's design was unbelievably badly coordinated, with a front end that appeared to emanate from a conventional estate car (station wagon), and a rear that hailed from an SUV – albeit one that had been squashed. This was Buick's attempt at getting buyers to shun established German marques such as Audi and BMW, but all it did was confirm that, while Teutonic styling was rarely anything other than understated, it was at least in good taste. Unsurprisingly, the Signia's styling went down like a lead balloon, and no elements from it reached production.

SPECIFICATION

ORIGIN	USA
DEBUT	Detroit 1998
ENGINE CAPACITY	3800cc (232cu in) supercharged
CONFIGURATION	Front-mounted V6
TRANSMISSION	Four-speed auto, part-time four-wheel drive
POWER	179kW (240bhp)
TOP SPEED	N/A
LENGTH	4705mm (185in)
WIDTH	1886mm (74in)

Left: *The Signia was intended to be multi-talented, offering the luxury of a saloon (sedan), the versatility of a van and the practicality of an SUV.*

At the push of a button, the car's rear load bay extended outwards by 38cm (15in), to aid loading and unloading.

Infrared sensors in the vehicle's pillars could detect vehicles in the Signia's blind spots, signalling a warning in the rearview mirrors.

The instrumentation was projected onto the windscreen via a head-up display – or onto the centre console in the same way.

Signia users would press a button for the climate control, seats, steering wheel and sound system to be set to preconfigured settings.

CHEVROLET BISCAYNE (1955)

In the history of close shaves, few could have led to more sighs of relief than the Biscayne not going into production after its 1955 unwrapping. The only things that survived from this concept were the new V8 engine and the name; there would be production Chevrolets bearing Biscayne badges from the 1959 model year. This was another one of those concepts where you wonder why the designers did not spend an extra few hours coming up with something that did not make you feel sick every time you laid eyes on it. After all, how long could it possibly take to come up with a nose less gruesome than the one shown here?

SPECIFICATION

ORIGIN	USA
DEBUT	Motorama 1955
ENGINE CAPACITY	4.3 litres (262cu in)
CONFIGURATION	Front-mounted V8
TRANSMISSION	Three-speed auto, rear-wheel drive
POWER	160kW (215bhp)
TOP SPEED	N/A
LENGTH	N/A
WIDTH	N/A

Left: GM claimed that this four-door four-seater pillarless hardtop was an 'exploration in elegance'. The auto giant clearly had a different perspective from everyone else.

The windscreen featured its own name: 'Astro-dome'. This was down to the fact that it was blended into the front of the roof panel.

To keep weight down, resist rust, lower crash repair costs and ease manufacture, the bodyshell was made of fibreglass.

As was common practice in the world of concept cars at the time, the front seats swivelled to allow easier entry and exit.

Despite that ugly nose, the rest of the Biscayne was not too bad – which was a blessing because it previewed Chevrolet's designs for the late 1950s and beyond.

CHRYSLER TURBOFLITE (1961)

Here it is: definitive proof that beauty is clearly in the eye of the beholder. After all, when the Turboflite was conceived, somebody somewhere must have held it in some affection and felt that it pressed all the right buttons for style and panache – even though it clearly didn't. Designed in-house but built by Ghia, the Turboflite was the first of Chrysler's turbine concept cars – it was reckoned that the gas turbine was the way forwards when it came to motive power for roadgoing passenger cars. But such engines are inherently very thirsty and hard to tame, even though they are incredibly smooth – so we are unlikely to see production gas turbine-powered cars any time soon.

SPECIFICATION

ORIGIN	USA
DEBUT	1961
ENGINE CAPACITY	N/A
CONFIGURATION	Front-mounted CR-2-A gas turbine
TRANSMISSION	Three-speed auto, rear-wheel drive
POWER	104kW (140bhp)
TOP SPEED	N/A
LENGTH	N/A
WIDTH	N/A

Left: *Chrysler's Turboflite concept featured perhaps the most complicated door of any car ever. A conventional lower door was opened, activating a canopy above, which then raised automatically.*

Inside there were four seats made of trimmed satin-finished aluminium and cantilevered off a centrally mounted spine.

The rear spoiler was more than just a little bit obvious, but it was not just for high-speed stability; it also acted as an air brake under heavy deceleration.

The canopy incorporated a wraparound windscreen along with hinged windows for the passengers; it was not possible to use conventional windows.

Above the waistline the Turboflite was seriously ugly, but the nose, with those exposed front wheels, was also fantastically repulsive.

CHRYSLER CROSSFIRE (2001)

If you thought the production Crossfire was a bit of a dog – and even if you didn't – the original concept was even worse. In theory that suggests that Chrysler at least listened to somebody before building thousands of production cars – but whoever signed off the original concept clearly had no idea of what constitutes good design. The nose did not work, the proportions were all wrong and from the back it looked like a hunchback. By the time the car went into production, Chrysler had fixed the first problem – but then it must have run out of time, patience or money. Or, most likely, all three.

SPECIFICATION

ORIGIN	USA
DEBUT	Detroit 2001
ENGINE CAPACITY	2.7 litres (165cu in) supercharged
CONFIGURATION	Front-mounted V6
TRANSMISSION	Five-speed manual, rear-wheel drive
POWER	205kW (275bhp)
TOP SPEED	238km/h (148mph)
LENGTH	3972mm (156in)
WIDTH	1839mm (72in)

Left: *Production Crossfires would be conventionally constructed; the concept, though, featured a carbon-fibre bodyshell on an alloy chassis.*

Harking back to the 1940s and 1950s, there was a split windscreen front and rear, plus a 'spine' that ran the length of the car.

While production Crossfires would have a 3.2-litre (195cu in) Mercedes V6 engine, the concept featured a 2.7-litre (165cu in) version of the same powerplant.

The wheelbase was long for such a short car, ensuring that the front and rear overhangs were very short.

One of the best exterior details was the wheel design; those eight-spoke alloys measured 48cm (19in) across at the front and 53cm (21in) at the back.

CITROËN C-CROSSER (2001)

Citroën was once renowned for its innovative and beautiful car design, so where did it all go wrong? How could the same company that produced the DS come up with something as disjointed as the C-Crosser, the vehicle that nobody in their right mind could possibly ever want? Perhaps therein lies the answer; maybe Citroën aimed the car at those who were more than just a little unhinged. Certainly its designers were; here was a vehicle that could morph from a six-seater people carrier to a 'semi-roadster' (whatever that is) or pick-up. Useful maybe, but when a vehicle looks like this it is pretty obvious Citroën was on a fast road to nowhere.

SPECIFICATION

ORIGIN	France
DEBUT	Frankfurt 2001
ENGINE CAPACITY	2 litres (122cu in)
CONFIGURATION	Front-mounted four-cylinder
TRANSMISSION	Automatic, four-wheel drive
POWER	N/A
TOP SPEED	N/A
LENGTH	4280mm (169in)
WIDTH	N/A

Left: *At the touch of a button, the glass roof and tailgate of the C-Crosser slid into the rear floor; stowing the rear seats as well created a pick-up configuration.*

There was four-wheel steering, and at high speeds the rear wheels turned in the same direction as the fronts, for increased stability.

Drive-by-wire technology created a seriously uncluttered cabin, with linkages eradicated. That meant better safety and greater comfort.

Hydractive 3 suspension allowed the C-Crosser to be raised or lowered by up to 60mm (2.36in), giving a maximum ground clearance of 150mm (six inches).

A 2-litre (122cu in) engine drove all four wheels via an automatic transmission. The Electronic Stability Programme was also fitted.

DAIHATSU MIDGET IV (1997)

Daihatsu chose the perfect name for this concept because the vehicle's talents were so tiny as to be barely perceptible. These nasty little machines were shown under the slogan of 'compact magic', and Daihatsu would have pulled off a neat trick if it could have persuaded anybody to part with good money for one of them. Ugly and badly proportioned, the Midget IV featured such excruciatingly bad styling that it was painful to look at. Still, if you consider some of the oddities that have come out of Japan over the years, the Midget may well have found a market in its homeland.

SPECIFICATION

ORIGIN	Japan
DEBUT	Tokyo 1997
ENGINE CAPACITY	660cc (40cu in)
CONFIGURATION	Front-mounted three-cylinder
TRANSMISSION	Three-speed auto, front-wheel drive
POWER	N/A
TOP SPEED	N/A
LENGTH	2990mm (118in)
WIDTH	1335mm (53in)

Left: *Despite the seating layout (one in the front; two in the back), the Midget IV's three doors were arranged with one on each side of the driver's seat, and just one at the back (on the nearside) for those in the rear.*

There was seating for three; the driver on his own in the front and two seats, very close together, in the rear.

Although the front track looks much wider than the rear, the difference is just 35mm (1.38in) because of the heavily tapered bodyshell.

The Midget was designed to fit into Japan's K-Class, which is why it was so small and packed a mere 660cc (40cu in) engine.

As well as the three-seat passenger version, Daihatsu also engineered a commercial Midget IV, for carrying very small quantities of goods.

DODGE NEON EXPRESSO *(1994)*

Anything that featured 'Neon' as part of its name was guaranteed to be bad news; this was one of Dodge's least accomplished production cars ever. What made the Expresso even worse was that it looked like something driven straight out of a cartoon, with bizarre curves everywhere, from the bodywork to the windows. With a design inspired by 'big-city taxis', the Expresso was billed as a redesign of the family taxi – but with Dodge claiming that the 'concept was based on the platform of the fun-to-drive Neon', you just knew this was a vehicle that had less than zero credibility.

SPECIFICATION

ORIGIN	USA
DEBUT	Detroit 1994
ENGINE CAPACITY	2 litres (122cu in)
CONFIGURATION	Front-mounted four-cylinder
TRANSMISSION	Three-speed auto, front-wheel drive
POWER	98kW (132bhp)
TOP SPEED	N/A
LENGTH	3597mm (142in)
WIDTH	1679mm (66in)

Left: *The Expresso's bright yellow paintwork and bubble-inspired design were supposed to make you feel good; all they did instead was to make you feel slightly nauseated.*

The Expresso's interior features included an underfloor storage area, as well as an integrated satellite navigation system.

Motive power was provided by a Neon-sourced four-cylinder engine. Displacing 2 litres (122cu in), it could generate 98kW (132bhp).

Based on a production Neon platform (guaranteeing mediocre dynamics), the Expresso was 61cm (24in) shorter but 38cm (15in) taller.

A laptop computer in the back of the driver's seat provided rear-seat occupants with limited amounts of entertainment.

FIAT X1/23 CITY CAR (1972)

The 1970s were a pretty miserable decade all round, what with mass unemployment, high inflation and generally terrible design of everything from carpets to cars. As if that weren't enough, Fiat decided to unveil its City Car concept, later badged the X1/23. While Fiat's greatest cars have all been minnows, this was not one of its best efforts; the proportions were just plain wrong and the lines were nothing less than horrific. Still, at least Fiat never progressed the idea, sticking instead to its 126 and 127 to keep small car fans happy. Let's be thankful for small mercies.

SPECIFICATION	
ORIGIN	Italy
DEBUT	Turin 1972
ENGINE CAPACITY	Electric
CONFIGURATION	Front-mounted electric motor
TRANSMISSION	Front-wheel drive
POWER	10kW (13.5bhp)
TOP SPEED	75km/h (47mph)
LENGTH	2642mm (104in)
WIDTH	1510mm (59in)

Left: *When it was first unveiled in 1972, the City Car was a non-runner. In 1973 Fiat unveiled an electric edition and badged the concept as the X1/23.*

With an overall length of just 2.6m (104in), it is no surprise that there was seating for just two with a token bit of luggage space thrown in for good measure.

The X1/23's range was just 72km (45 miles) at a steady 50km/h (31mph). Power came from nickel-zinc batteries instead of the more usual lead-acid items.

This may have been a tiny city car, but it still tipped the scales at a very hefty 822kg (1812lb) – 168kg (370lb) of which was the battery pack.

With that swooping windowline, the side windows could not be lowered. To keep the cabin cool, air conditioning was provided, further reducing the car's range.

GHIA SELENE (1959)

While some Italian styling houses produced one masterpiece after another throughout the 1950s, most of Ghia's hits were punctuated by a series of hopeless misses. The Selene was one of them; it followed on from the Gilda and Dart, which were reasonably inoffensive, even if they were hardly groundbreaking. The Selene was the combined work of the head of Ghia's design division Sergio Sartorelli and designer Tom Tjaarda, who was to become one of Ghia's main stylists. The car was born from a fascination with aircraft design, with cruising speeds of the then-current passenger jets reaching previously unimaginable levels. For some reason, however, the Selene appears to have been designed back to front, leaving onlookers not knowing whether the car is coming or going.

SPECIFICATION

ORIGIN	Italy
DEBUT	1959
ENGINE CAPACITY	N/A
CONFIGURATION	Mid-engined
TRANSMISSION	N/A
POWER	N/A
TOP SPEED	N/A
LENGTH	N/A
WIDTH	N/A

Left: *The Selene was penned between Sergio Sartorelli and Tom Tjaarda. They were clearly each working on a front end and forgot to produce a rear.*

No engine was fitted to the Selene, but if there had it would have been a simple petrol (gasoline) unit fitted towards the rear.

There was seating for six, with two chairs provided up front and another four behind, between the axles and facing each other.

As was typical at the time, there was nothing so boring as a wheel with which to steer; instead there was a W-shaped set of handlebars.

With particularly challenging styling, the Selene looks as if it is driving backwards. That massive front overhang would also no doubt have provided an especially interesting driving experience.

GHIA SELENE SECONDA *(1960)*

Proving that even respected styling houses do not always learn from the most stupid of mistakes, Ghia came back for more with its second take on the Selene. As with its predecessor, the Selene II featured an extremely aerodynamic profile, largely inspired by aircraft design. When Ghia introduced the Ghia in the early 1960s, it claimed that this was the type of car that everyone would be driving within a decade. While it's true that we would all need cars that were fast, safe, efficient and stylish, the Selene II clearly could not deliver all those things. Indeed, if you take another look at it, you might think that maybe the Ford Cortina Mk3 was not so bad after all.

SPECIFICATION

ORIGIN	Italy
DEBUT	1960
ENGINE CAPACITY	1.0–2.5 litres (61–153cu in)
CONFIGURATION	Mid-mounted
TRANSMISSION	N/A
POWER	N/A
TOP SPEED	N/A
LENGTH	4780mm (188in)
WIDTH	1880mm (74in)

Left: *As with the first Selene, there was a massive front overhang, but the wheelbase was not especially long, guaranteeing atrocious handling characteristics.*

Seemingly in a bid to offer as little crash protection as possible, the engine was mounted at the back. No powerplant was suggested because this was a non-runner.

The Selene Seconda offered just three seats; the driver sat alone in a central seat, while the two passengers sat behind, facing towards the rear.

Running the length of the Selene Seconda's rear deck was a tail fin; it was in place with the sole aim of optimizing stability at high speeds.

The cab-forward stance was designed to maximize visibility for the driver, while also evening out overall weight distribution.

HEULIEZ PREGUNTA (1998)

Perhaps the most tragic of all concepts are those that take a perfectly good car and turn it into something that you really would not want to be seen looking at, never mind sitting in. The Pregunta was just such a creation; it took a Lamborghini Diablo and reshaped it to create this horrendous monstrosity. The French coachbuilder Heuliez was noted for its awkward conversions on various cars, especially icons such as the Citroën SM, but the Pregunta possibly marked an all-time low. Had the car made small-series production, it is highly doubtful any would have sold; the sole car constructed has passed into private hands.

SPECIFICATION

ORIGIN	France
DEBUT	Paris 1998
ENGINE CAPACITY	5707cc (348cu in)
CONFIGURATION	Mid-mounted V12
TRANSMISSION	Five-speed manual, rear-wheel drive
POWER	395kW (530bhp)
TOP SPEED	335km/h (208mph)
LENGTH	4516mm (178in)
WIDTH	2084mm (82in)

Left: ***With lines inspired by fighter aircraft, the Heuliez Pregunta was intended to instantly convey the impression of supersonic flight to anyone who looked at it.***

Just as with the donor car, there were scissor-style doors that hinged forwards and upwards at the same time.

The Pregunta took the Lamborghini Diablo's mechanicals and used them unchanged – meaning it packed a 5.7-litre (348cu in) V12 engine.

The Pregunta took its name from the Spanish for 'question'. The most obvious question anybody would ask after seeing this is 'why'?

The car's interior was packed with high-tech gadgetry; the Formula 1-style dashboard was constructed by Magnetti-Marelli.

HONDA NEUKOM (1999)

Take one greenhouse and add wheels – and hey presto! One Honda Neukom to go. Offering all the style and aerodynamics of a potting shed, the Neukom was 'developed around the totally new concept of creating a car to serve as the transporter of an open space for social enjoyment". Clearly the folks at Honda spent more time trying to come up with an excuse for the Neukom than they spent designing it. At least it was nicer inside than out, though, with a light, airy cabin and great access, thanks to large doors and a split tailgate. Nonetheless, there is no denying that it was still a horrifically bad concept …

SPECIFICATION

ORIGIN	Japan
DEBUT	Tokyo 1999
ENGINE CAPACITY	N/A
CONFIGURATION	Front-mounted
TRANSMISSION	Probably automatic, front-wheel drive
POWER	N/A
TOP SPEED	N/A
LENGTH	3500mm (138in)
WIDTH	1800mm (71in)

Left: *Each of the Neukom's seats featured a four-point harness; the chairs were made of wood, 'to make communication more comfortable,' according to Honda.*

A series of louvres in the glass roof slid to each side – with electric assistance, naturally – to open up the cabin to the elements.

The main aesthetic problem lay in the ridiculously low waistline, with the glass making up more than half of the car's height.

To maximize interior space, the Neukom's wheels were pushed to the corners to ensure as long a wheelbase as possible.

No powerplant was proposed, but with so little space available it would have had to be small and mounted in the nose.

HONDA FUYA-JO *(1999)*

As if one seriously badly judged concept weren't enough, Honda managed to unveil another scarily atrocious offering at the 1999 Tokyo motor show – the Fuya-jo. Looking like a cross between an armoured car and a supermarket trolley, the Fuya-jo featured a minimal glasshouse and wheels that looked as if they had been stolen from a Lego set. Set up as a music station on wheels, the Fuya-jo did not appear to be a runner; no motive power was mentioned. Whatever was fitted, given the space available, it would likely have produced less power than the stereo in the car's cabin.

SPECIFICATION

ORIGIN	Japan
DEBUT	Tokyo 1999
ENGINE CAPACITY	N/A
CONFIGURATION	Front-mounted
TRANSMISSION	Probably automatic, front-wheel drive
POWER	N/A
TOP SPEED	N/A
LENGTH	3050mm (120in)
WIDTH	1650mm (65in)

Left: *The Fuya-jo's travelling-party theme could not be avoided. The switchgear looked like a club DJ's mixing desk, while the steering wheel resembled a DJ's turntable.*

The Fuya-jo took its name from a Japanese expression meaning 'a town that never sleeps' – apparently it was meant to party like one too.

The interior was set up like a mobile discotheque, with speakers galore and a major sound system installed.

Each of the four occupants travelled 'perched' rather than seated, like sitting at a bar in a nightclub. Great for comfort and safety …

Each seat was fitted with a four-point seatbelt, while there was a skateboard rack incorporated into the rear door.

HYUNDAI FGV-II (1999)

FGV stood for 'Future Green Vehicle', but somehow you just know by looking at this car that, if this represented the future of motoring, walking, cycling and taking the bus would suddenly become very popular. Crawling 300 miles on your hands and knees would have been preferable to being seen in this abomination. As the name suggests, the FGV-II was the follow-up to the FGV, a hybrid compact SUV not nearly as offensive as its successor. You could be forgiven for thinking that Hyundai's designers must have had a heavy night on the town before coming up with this creation. Whatever the case, it was not their finest hour.

SPECIFICATION

ORIGIN	Korea
DEBUT	Seoul 1999
ENGINE CAPACITY	N/A
CONFIGURATION	Front-mounted engine
TRANSMISSION	Automatic, front-wheel drive
POWER	N/A
TOP SPEED	177km/h (110mph)
LENGTH	4385mm (173in)
WIDTH	1765mm (69in)

Left: *The FGV-II was designed as a response to California's Zero Emissions Vehicle (ZEV) Mandate, demanding ultra-clean cars in an effort to improve air quality and decrease greenhouse emissions.*

Regardless of the technology underneath, nobody could take a car this ugly very seriously. That back end was just plain wrong.

There was seating for four inside, each occupant having their own fully sculpted leather-trimmed chair.

A petrol (gasoline) engine was assisted by an electric motor to give performance with economy; it was claimed up to 2.94 litres per 100km (80mpg) was possible.

At low speeds the FGV-II was propelled using electricity only; only when cruising or accelerating would the petrol (gasoline) engine cut in.

ITALDESIGN CAPSULA (1982)

It is not uncommon for a design house to set out with a perfectly good aim, only to execute it in the most clumsy fashion imaginable. Step forwards the Capsula from Italdesign. When the Italian outfit decided to create a platform on which pretty much any type of vehicle could be based, it sounded like a great proposal. Then it ended up with this – one of the most disjointed car designs ever. With a glasshouse that stretched down almost to the floor and a bonnet (hood) line at the same level, the Capsula looked as if it would topple over at the first corner. Back to the drawing board, then.

SPECIFICATION

ORIGIN	Italy
DEBUT	Turin 1982
ENGINE CAPACITY	1490cc (91cu in)
CONFIGURATION	Front-mounted flat-four
TRANSMISSION	Five-speed manual, front-wheel drive
POWER	78kW (105bhp)
TOP SPEED	N/A
LENGTH	3720mm (146in)
WIDTH	1770mm (70in)

Left: *Even though the Capsula was less than four metres (12½ft) long, the cabin was exceptionally spacious; 80 per cent of the car's length was for its occupants.*

s well as this passenger car, other bodystyles proposed for the Capsula included a beach buggy, van and various commercials.

That lower tier of glass, below the windows and windscreen, was to allow the car to be positioned more easily when manoeuvring.

Because the platform was to be used for a wide variety of vehicle types, it could be front-wheel drive or four-wheel drive.

The Capsula's engine was borrowed from the Alfa Romeo Alfasud, so it was a 1.5-litre (91cu in) four-cylinder boxer engine.

ITALDESIGN 20/20 *(2001)*

If you stopped 100 people in the street and asked them to name the most beautiful car ever made, the chances are the Aston Martin DB7 would feature fairly high on the list. Unless it had had a makeover courtesy of Italdesign, of course. For some reason, this Italian styling house felt the need to take a perfectly good DB7 and butcher it to come up with the truly awful creation you see here. Somehow the outfit had the gall to proclaim the 20/20 a 'meticulously calibrated piece of engineering' – it may have been beautifully constructed, but with looks like that all the precision in the world would not have made any difference. It was still a mess.

SPECIFICATION

ORIGIN	Italy
DEBUT	Geneva 2001
ENGINE CAPACITY	5935cc (362cu in)
CONFIGURATION	Front-mounted V12
TRANSMISSION	Six-speed manual, rear-wheel drive
POWER	373kW (500bhp)
TOP SPEED	N/A
LENGTH	4455mm (175in)
WIDTH	1900mm (75in)

Left: *All of the 20/20's mechanicals were carried over from the DB7 donor car, which meant a 5.9-litre (362cu in) V12 engine and a six-speed manual gearbox.*

The aluminium structure was displayed prominently, hence the metallic roll bar, windscreen surround and sills.

The rest of the panels were made of carbon-fibre and fibreglass; Italdesign resisted the temptation to leave the former unpainted.

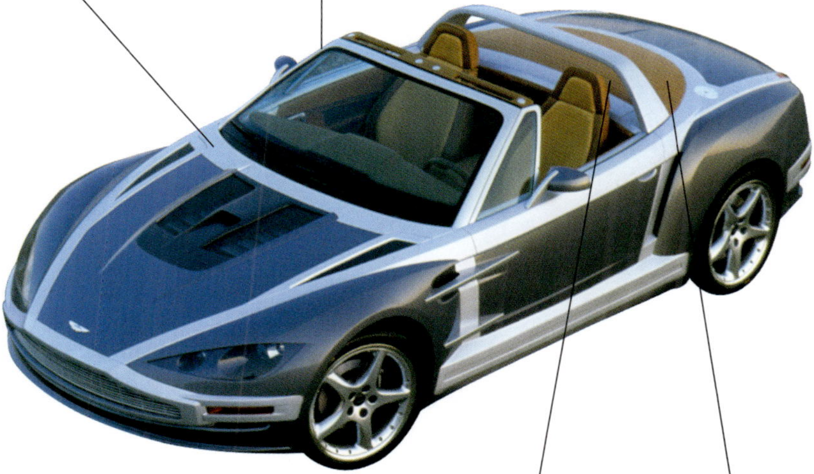

There was usually space for two seats only, but if the roll bar and rear deck were removed two more seats could be fitted in.

There was also plenty of extruded aluminium inside the 20/20's cabin, plus lashings of leather trim and lots of wood inserts.

ITALDESIGN COLUMBUS (1992)

A luxurious minibus powered by a V12 engine sounds like something very tasty indeed. When you wrap it up in a bodyshell that looks like a jet aircraft that has crashed into a people-carrier, however, suddenly it's not so good. The name may have suggested nothing more than a cringeworthy play on words, but the Columbus was actually created to celebrate the 500th anniversary of Christopher Columbus discovering America. That would be the America that likes everything on the XXXL side, then – although even the most ardent fan of supersizing would baulk at the sight of this toe-curling creation. Big it may have undeniably been, but it certainly was not beautiful.

SPECIFICATION

ORIGIN	Italy
DEBUT	Turin 1992
ENGINE CAPACITY	5000cc (305cu in)
CONFIGURATION	Mid-mounted V12
TRANSMISSION	Five-speed manual, four-wheel drive
POWER	224kW (300bhp)
TOP SPEED	232km/h (144mph)
LENGTH	5997mm (236in)
WIDTH	2190mm (86in)

Left: *The Columbus's driver sat in the middle, high up, with all of the passenger seats arranged in pairs behind. The front three seats were higher than the rest.*

All four wheels were driven via a five-speed manual gearbox. There was also four-wheel steering and all-round independent suspension.

The V12 engine, sourced from a BMW 8-Series, sat in the centre of the Columbus – hardly what could be called the height of practicality.

In standard form seven people could be accommodated; two extra seats were available if needed, or they could all be removed to create a van.

There were two doors on each side, with the whole bodyshell manufactured in carbon-fibre to keep weight down and the strength up.

MERCEDES BIONIC CAR (2005)

Basing your car's design on a fish might seem like madness, but it is really not such a bad idea. After all, fish are aerodynamic and can be a very attractive shape, as well as very colourful. But then there is the box fish, which is possibly the ugliest creature ever devised by nature. So guess which fish Mercedes decided to model its Bionic Car on? You got it: the box fish, with its ugly high forehead and badly proportioned body. So while Mercedes managed to create one of the most aerodynamic automotive forms ever, there was no way anybody would ever want to be seen in one of these repulsive creations.

SPECIFICATION

ORIGIN	Germany
DEBUT	Washington 2005
ENGINE CAPACITY	1991cc (121cu in) turbocharged
CONFIGURATION	Front-mounted diesel four-cylinder
TRANSMISSION	CVT, front-wheel drive
POWER	103kW (138bhp)
TOP SPEED	190km/h (118mph)
LENGTH	4243mm (167in)
WIDTH	1815mm (71in)

Left: *The roof of the Bionic Car consisted of as much glass as possible, to lighten the vehicle's interior. Lighting was by LED, while exterior door handles popped out electrically.*

It may have been ugly, but this was one slippery shape; the Bionic Car had a drag coefficient of just 0.19, far better than any production car.

Cleaning up the exhaust was a system called Selective Catalytic Reduction, which reduced nitrogen oxide emissions by 80 per cent.

Power came from a direct-injection 2.0-litre (121cu in) turbodiesel engine, driving the front wheels via a continuously variable transmission.

The aerodynamics and light weight ensured great efficiency; 65 miles could be squeezed out of a gallon of fuel (3.62 litres per 100km).

MERCEDES F700 *(2007)*

Mercedes-Benz has had more time than anyone to perfect its design. After all, the German company was building cars before anybody else, so with more than a century of car production under its belt you would have thought it would always get things right. Clearly you would be wrong, though, because this concept packed in the luxury, the safety and the space – but it most definitely did not have the style. A pair of oversized headlights flanked an equally badly proportioned grille, while the plunging waistline made the car look like a badly executed cut and shut. Perhaps another century will allow Mercedes to get the hang of things.

SPECIFICATION

ORIGIN	Germany
DEBUT	Frankfurt 2007
ENGINE CAPACITY	1.8 litres (110cu in) twin-turbo
CONFIGURATION	Front-mounted petrol (gasoline)–diesel in-line four
TRANSMISSION	Seven-speed auto
POWER	177kW (238bhp)
TOP SPEED	200km/h (125mph)
LENGTH	5180mm (204in)
WIDTH	1960mm (77in)

Left: *At least with Mercedes' F700 there was no chance of rear-seat passengers getting bored, thanks to a 50cm (20in) TV screen and surround-sound audio system.*

An interface allowed front-seat occupants to personalize the F700's functions, while the instrumentation was projected onto the windscreen.

A laser system allowed the F700 to scan the road ahead, adjusting the suspension according to what it saw.

The power source was truly revolutionary, as the DiesOtto engine could run on petrol (gasoline) or diesel, offering both performance and economy.

The rear seats were asymmetric; there were two opposing chairs on the right and one conventional item on the left.

MITSUBISHI ESR (1993)

Mitsubishi was ahead of the game when it launched its ESR concept in 1993. The name was an abbreviation of 'Ecological Science Research', with the vehicle a test-bed for green technologies. All very laudable, of course, but why is it necessary for any car to ever be this ugly? The car could have generated energy as it drove along, but that still would not have excused it for being such a blot on the landscape. From the front the ESR looked OK, but from all other angles it was a tragic mess – the designers initially chose a one-box design, then chickened out at the last minute, going for a notchback. And to think that they were so close to greatness …

SPECIFICATION

ORIGIN	Japan
DEBUT	Tokyo 1993
ENGINE CAPACITY	1.5 litres (92cu in) turbocharged
CONFIGURATION	Rear-mounted four-cylinder
TRANSMISSION	Three-speed auto, four-wheel drive
POWER	70kW (94bhp) (plus 20kW/27bhp from the petrol (gasoline) engine)
TOP SPEED	200km/h (125mph)
LENGTH	4535mm (179in)
WIDTH	1725mm (68in)

Left: *To minimize the amount of energy needed to run the ESR, it was incredibly aerodynamic (the vehicle's drag coefficient was 0.25) and light too.*

The interior was not especially high-tech, but it was very uncluttered. There was seating for four, with airbags and three-point seatbelts for everyone.

The wheels were always driven by an electric motor, powered by batteries that were topped up from a mains supply.

Topping up the batteries on the move, if necessary, was a 1.5-litre (92cu in) water-cooled twin-spark four-cylinder engine.

Other ways in which the batteries were recharged on the move was by the fitment of regenerative braking, plus roof-mounted solar panels.

MITSUBISHI SUP *(2002)*

It packed about five bodystyles and two power sources into one concept, so it is no wonder that the SUP, or Sports Utility Pack, looked somewhat confused. With both petrol (gasoline) and electric powertrains stowed away, plus a mixture of SUV, convertible, MPV, sportscar and family cars, the SUP in theory offered something for everyone. Or, as Mitsubishi put it, the SUP was 'for nature lovers who are happy using hi-tech gadgets and gizmos Monday to Friday; then out for a bunch of fun communing with nature at weekends and holidays'. Seemed they were hedging their bets as to who would buy it. In reality, the answer would have been nobody, of course.

SPECIFICATION

ORIGIN	Japan
DEBUT	Detroit 2002
ENGINE CAPACITY	1999cc (122cu in)
CONFIGURATION	Front-mounted four-cylinder
TRANSMISSION	Automatic, part-time four-wheel drive
POWER	N/A
TOP SPEED	N/A
LENGTH	4166mm (164in)
WIDTH	1854mm (73in)

Left: ***Mitsubishi claimed that the SUP was aimed at 'young, tech-savvy urbanites' – this demographic must have been identified as having no discernbile taste.***

One of the key features of the SUP was that it was a convertible; a closed edition was unveiled at the 2001 Tokyo motor show.

The angle of the windscreen was ridiculously shallow; front-seat passengers were likely to gouge themselves on the header rail when getting in or out.

The SUP looked a bit odd with the roof down, but once the roof was raised the car looked really awkward because of the very bulky back end.

A petrol (gasoline) engine drove the front wheels, while electric motors drove the rear wheels when extra urge or traction was required.

PACKARD PREDICTOR (1956)

Seen more than half a century on, the Predictor looks nothing less than horrifically ugly – a mishmash of jarring lines. But when this last-ditch attempt to save Packard was unveiled in 1956, it was greeted with enthusiasm by the media and public alike, who loved its looks and neat details. Still – what did they know? They clearly had not realized that that chintzy grille stuck onto an otherwise restrained nose (albeit with pop-up headlights) was the height of bad taste. That reverse-rake rear window was also a styling disaster, while the rear lights were ridiculously oversized. No wonder Packard went belly-up soon after.

SPECIFICATION

ORIGIN	USA
DEBUT	Chicago 1956
ENGINE CAPACITY	5766cc (352cu in)
CONFIGURATION	Front-mounted V8
TRANSMISSION	Two-speed auto, rear-wheel drive
POWER	194kW (260bhp)
TOP SPEED	N/A
LENGTH	5639mm (222in)
WIDTH	2159mm (85in)

Left: *As with most concepts, the Predictor was based on an existing chassis – in this case a stretched Packard Clipper item, with a 3100mm (122in) wheelbase.*

The roof panels over the front seats slid into the fixed panel behind when the doors were opened, to aid entry and exit.

There was surprisingly little chrome on the Predictor's bodywork – Packard reckoned that the future of car design lay in cleaner styling.

Another gimmick incorporated to ease entry and exit was swivelling seats, which spun around when the doors were opened.

Under the bonnet (hood) was a 5766cc (352cu in) overhead-valve cast-iron V8, pumping out 515Nm (380lbf ft) of torque.

PONTIAC AZTEK (1999)

Of all the concept cars ever unveiled, the Aztek must rate as one of the ugliest – a view with which the entire world seemed to agree when the car debuted in 1999. Despite this, Pontiac reckoned it would make sense to put the car into production – virtually unchanged. So, buyers could choose from a range of SUVs that offered (in many cases) good looks with a decent level of off-road ability. Or you could buy an Aztek that scrabbled about in the rough looking like a pregnant rhinoceros. In the end, it was not really all that much of a choice to make …

SPECIFICATION

ORIGIN	USA
DEBUT	Detroit 1999
ENGINE CAPACITY	3.4 litres (207cu in)
CONFIGURATION	Front-mounted V6
TRANSMISSION	Four-speed auto, front-wheel drive
POWER	149kW (200bhp)
TOP SPEED	180km/h (112mph)
LENGTH	4546mm (179in)
WIDTH	1956mm (77in)

Left: ***The Aztek's cabin was a relief after the outside. It was tastefully trimmed in sombre colours with yellow highlights to lift things.***

It looks hideously disfigured from this angle, but you can choose any view of the Aztek and it is not any more flattering.

Up front was a 3.4-litre (207cu in) V6 engine, the power from which was fed to all four wheels via a four-speed automatic gearbox.

The bonnet (hood) of the Aztek appeared to have been designed to fit an altogether different car. It resembled a rhinoceros, it was so ungainly.

Although this vehicle was supposedly an off-roader, its monocoque construction and minimal ground clearance meant that it was incapable in the rough.

RUSSO BALTIQUE IMPRESSION

In 1907 Russo Baltique sprang to life, to build highly exclusive cars for the very wealthy. The cars were made in tiny numbers, but were of a very high quality. A century after the marque was inaugurated, some bright spark decided that it should be revived. Going by the Impression, however, they really should not have bothered. With lines inspired by coachbuilt cars of the 1930s, the Impression mixed old and new to terrible effect. It is no wonder that nothing more was heard of the company after this concept was unveiled in spring 2007. Amazingly, the Impression was offered for sale if anyone was interested in parting with their hard-earned cash. They weren't, of course.

SPECIFICATION

ORIGIN	Russia
DEBUT	Geneva 2007
ENGINE CAPACITY	5513cc (336cu in) twin-turbo
CONFIGURATION	Front-mounted V12
TRANSMISSION	Six-speed auto
POWER	414kW (555bhp)
TOP SPEED	315km/h (196mph) (claimed)
LENGTH	5500mm (217in)
WIDTH	1880mm (74in)

Left: *The dashboard was made from a single piece of the threatened African hardwood Zebrano; the steering wheel and door trims were made from the same exotic timber.*

Up to three cars could be made annually, with no more than 15 to be made in all. Unsurprisingly, none was ever actually constructed.

Motive power was provided by a twin-turbo Maybach-sourced 5.5-litre (336cu in) V12, so there was no shortage of grunt.

There was pneumatic suspension all round, with the Impression's ride height adjustable according to terrain and speed.

Those wheels were made specially for the Impression. They measured 508mm (20in) across and were made of aluminium alloy.

STOLA COUPÉ (2007)

This unnamed concept from Italian coachbuilder Stola was completely loopy and based on Maybach running gear – it was basically an even more extreme edition of the Maybach Exelero, not that you would think such a thing were possible. Stola aimed to offer 'no more than 25 examples' of the car, but it was obvious to anybody who clapped eyes on it that this was yet another concept that would never leave the starting blocks. One look at this and suddenly the Renault Avantime made sense. Perhaps even the SsangYong Rodius could justify itself. OK, then, definitely not the Rodius.

SPECIFICATION

ORIGIN	Italy
DEBUT	Geneva 2007
ENGINE CAPACITY	6.3 litres (384cu in) twin-turbo
CONFIGURATION	Front-mounted V12
TRANSMISSION	Five-speed manual, rear-wheel drive
POWER	559kW (750bhp)
TOP SPEED	In excess of 320km/h (200mph)
LENGTH	N/A
WIDTH	N/A

Left: *Stola was very optimistic where this coupé was concerned; the company claimed that this was to be just the first in a line of highly exclusive supercars.*

All of the Stola Coupé's running gear was taken straight from the Maybach, which meant a V12 engine and rear-wheel drive.

To ensure that customers did not feel shortchanged, Stola beefed up the twin-turbo V12 to give 559kW (750bhp) from 6.3 litres (384cu in).

Less successful design elements included the tacky-looking mascot perched on the nose, plus an electrically adjustable rear spoiler.

One of the most eye-catching features was the set of 559mm (22in) nine-spoke alloy wheels. They were shod with 315/25 tyres.

TOYOTA CX-80 *(1979)*

Car manufacturers often set out with good intentions, wanting to create a car that genuinely moves things on – then they go and mess it all up by coming up with a design so unspeakably grim that nobody could ever take it seriously. The CX-80 was just such a car; it was intended to offer ample space for a family of four, while taking up less road space than Toyota's smallest production model, the Starlet. It is a shame it looked as though the CX-80 had been designed by a young child – while wearing a blindfold. This really did represent an all-time low in Toyota's design catalogue.

SPECIFICATION

ORIGIN	Japan
DEBUT	Tokyo 1979
ENGINE CAPACITY	N/A
CONFIGURATION	Front-mounted
TRANSMISSION	Automatic, front-wheel drive
POWER	N/A
TOP SPEED	N/A
LENGTH	3531mm (139in)
WIDTH	N/A

Left: *Inside Toyota's CX-80, all of the instrumentation was digital; there was a hubless steering wheel and the automatic transmission was activated via buttons.*

The CX-80 made its debut at the 1979 Tokyo motor show, but by the time it arrived in Europe the next year it was called the FCX-80.

To make entry and exit easier, the car's doors tilted downwards once they had been opened, for greater clearance.

Toyota claimed that the CX-80 looked forwards to the end of the 1980s; it supposedly previewed how a city car would look then.

The headlights were mounted partway up the bonnet (hood), in a black pod, to prevent them being damaged in a low-speed bump.

TOYOTA RAUM *(1993)*

Toyota billed the Raum as a 'practical proposition for the next-generation family car' – but thankfully this prediction proved rather inaccurate. Sure, some car makers insisted on producing ill-proportioned and bland family transport throughout the 1990s, but even the worst were rarely as bad as this. Thanks to a ridiculously badly proportioned waistline, the Raum made its occupants look as though they were on display, with the car appearing like the sort of thing in which a head of state might go on an official parade. The problem with this was that the Raum did not possess any of the glitz it needed to carry out such a duty.

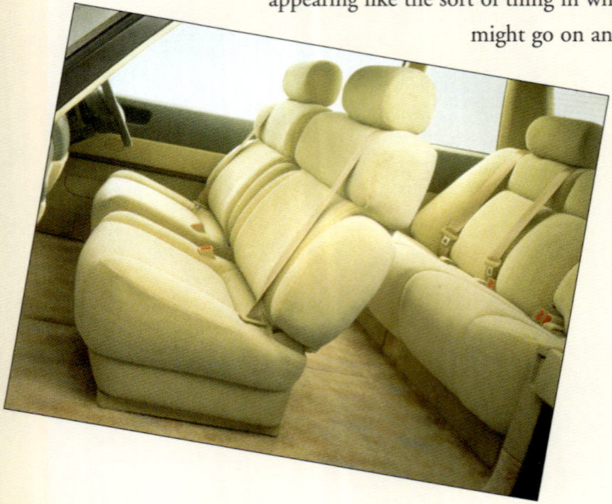

SPECIFICATION

ORIGIN	Japan
DEBUT	Frankfurt 1993
ENGINE CAPACITY	1800cc (110cu in)
CONFIGURATION	Front-mounted four-cylinder
TRANSMISSION	Four-speed auto, front-wheel drive
POWER	N/A
TOP SPEED	N/A
LENGTH	4000mm (157in)
WIDTH	1695mm (67in)

Left: ***The size of a small saloon (sedan), the Raum offered as much interior space as a limousine, according to Toyota.***

The Raum's deep, expansive glasshouse and low waistline made the vehicle look as if it had been inspired by a hearse.

Unusually, there was a single, very long door on each side that slid backwards to allow entry into the cabin.

One of the key features of the Raum was a lack of detailing to improve aerodynamics; everything was flush, from the glazing to the door handles.

In typical Japanese fashion, there were plenty of electronics on board, from a sat-nav system to a complicated audio set-up.

VALMET ZERONE (1999)

Valmet's expertise lay in building cars and designing convertible roof systems – but unfortunately not in designing whole cars. This lack proved to be the company's undoing because, when the wraps were taken off its Zerone concept at the 1999 Geneva motor show, nobody knew whether to applaud or laugh. Everyone assumed that this must be some kind of a practical joke, with the real concept set to pop up from underneath another cover. Sadly for Valmet, however, this was the real deal – the concept into which it had poured all of its energies in the hope that it would attract car makers wanting Valmet to build its cars for them. It is no surprise that the Zerone did not prove especially alluring and there were no takers.

SPECIFICATION

ORIGIN	Finland
DEBUT	Geneva 1999
ENGINE CAPACITY	Non-runner
CONFIGURATION	Front-mounted
TRANSMISSION	N/A
POWER	N/A
TOP SPEED	N/A
LENGTH	N/A
WIDTH	N/A

Left: *Safety was a key feature of the Valmet Zerone, with integral seatbelts for everyone. There were also pop-up roll hoops behind each of the seats.*

In Valmet's words, the Zerone was 'inspired by the classical GT cars of the 1960s and 1970s'. That'll be the very ugly ones, then.

The roof looked even worse than the car's front end, as it featured an ugly reverse-rake rear window, like the Ford Anglia of the 1960s.

The front and rear wings (fenders) both rose from a low point in the doors – a styling element that could never work successfully.

A gaping grille and a quartet of headlights made the Zerone look like a four-eyed fish in the process of breathing.

MINIMAL EFFORT

As with all art, car design should push the envelope – hopefully remaining within the boundaries of good taste. As you have already seen elsewhere in this book, there are plenty of cars that failed on the latter point, but there is also no shortage of concepts that failed on the former point too.

In this chapter you can read about the designs dreamed up during the lunch hour – the ones for which the bare minimum of effort was applied. These are the concepts which simply took a look at the past and rehashed it, supposedly for a modern age, or which took an existing car and grafted on a new face or bodystyle. Some of the laziest designs were those which tried to take an icon from the manufacturer's past, and re-introduce it for a new audience – concepts like the Ford 49, Lamborghini Miura and Fiat Trepiuno, but just as bad were those which did little more than take a standard production car and rework it slightly – cars like the Daewoo No. 1 or Bertone Jet2.

Left: *Take one Toyota Celica, stick on a couple of spoilers and call it a concept. Hardly groundbreaking...*

AUDI TT CLUBSPORT QUATTRO (2007)

You have one of the best-looking and most usable sportscars available, so what do you do? In Audi's case, you remove all the weather protection, stick on an aeroscreen and call it a concept. Weak did not even begin to sum up this abominable creation, which showed such a lack of creativity that it was embarrassing. How could a company renowned for its great concepts produce something this desperate? Despite this, Audi talked about limited production for the Clubsport – and no doubt if the company kept the numbers low enough, it would find the required number of speculators prepared to take a punt.

SPECIFICATION

ORIGIN	Germany
DEBUT	Wörthersee 2007
ENGINE CAPACITY	1984cc (121cu in) turbocharged
CONFIGURATION	Front-mounted four-cylinder
TRANSMISSION	Six-speed semi-auto, four-wheel drive
POWER	224kW (300bhp)
TOP SPEED	250km/h (155mph)
LENGTH	N/A
WIDTH	N/A

Left: *For the Clubsport Quattro's nose, Audi went for maximum aggression, hence the massive grille, plus huge ducts for brake cooling either side.*

Power was provided by a turbocharged 2-litre (121cu in) petrol engine, tuned to give 224kW (300bhp). This was sent to all four wheels via a DSG transmission.

There was no weather protection at all, while the windscreen was a speedster-type affair that could not accommodate any wipers.

The interior was typical Audi, with plenty of brushed alloy detailing. The seats were taken from the RS4, fitted with four-point harnesses.

Crash protection was poor because there was no A-pillar or roll bars – which is why mainstream production was not possible in this form.

BERTONE JET2 *(2004)*

If you were asked to name the most beautiful cars of all time, chances are you would come up with quite a few Aston Martins, and specifically the gorgeous Vanquish. With a bit of effort Aston Martin even created the stunning Rapide concept – a four-door saloon (sedan) based on the DB9. Judicious use of the imagination should have meant that a Vanquish estate (station wagon) would not prove too taxing. It would even fit in with the series of Aston Martin shooting brakes developed over the years by various coachbuilders, as well as Aston Martin itself. Like some of those conversions, however, the Jet2 was awkwardly styled – great from the front, but flair-free from the rear. And as the front was pretty much as Aston supplied it …

SPECIFICATION

ORIGIN	Italy
DEBUT	Geneva 2004
ENGINE CAPACITY	6000cc (366cu in)
CONFIGURATION	Front-mounted V12
TRANSMISSION	Six-speed semi-auto
POWER	336kW (450bhp)
TOP SPEED	305km/h (190mph) approx.
LENGTH	4675mm (184in)
WIDTH	1930mm (76in)

Left: *To prevent this estate car (station wagon) from looking too functional and pragmatic, its tailgate was sloped forwards to provide a sportier stance.*

The Jet2 was the sequel to a special-bodied Aston Martin DB4 GT, unveiled in 1961 – also made by Bertone.

Following a trend for show cars of the early twenty-first century, there was a glass roof fitted, to open up the cabin.

The rear side window was so short that this confection looked more like a compact hatchback than an estate car (station wagon).

The Jet2 may have looked surprisingly compact, but its wheelbase was stretched by 210mm (8¼in) over a conventional Vanquish coupé.

CHEVROLET TONKA TRUCK (1998)

Go to any monster truck race and you will see dozens of creations like this lined up, driving over old rusty old heaps and generally causing mayhem. So what possessed Chevrolet to come up with its own monster truck, built in-house but paraded as a concept car? Based on a 1999 Silverado, but unveiled at the 1998 custom-car fest that is the Las Vegas-based SEMA (Speciality Equipment Market Association) event, the Tonka was built in conjunction with the famous toy brand. As if this one were not bad enough, Tonka would go on to produce another concept, this time in conjunction with Ford, for the 2002 Detroit motor show.

SPECIFICATION

ORIGIN	USA
DEBUT	SEMA 1998
ENGINE CAPACITY	5967cc (364cu in)
CONFIGURATION	Front-mounted V8
TRANSMISSION	Four-speed auto, four-wheel drive
POWER	224kW (300bhp)
TOP SPEED	N/A
LENGTH	6261mm (246in)
WIDTH	1994mm (79in)

Left: *The focus was very much on turning the Silverado into a monster truck, so the Tonka had a standard 6-litre (364cu in) V8 engine.*

There were huge brush guard bars fitted to the front, below which was a winch in case the going got really slippery.

The biggest news with the Tonka was the jacked-up suspension, which allowed 1118mm (44in) tyres to be fitted at each corner.

Extra lighting was fitted to the roll bar fitted at the front of the pick-up bed, while a visor was installed above the windscreen.

To complete the effect, the Tonka was finished in plenty of garish primary colours just to make sure that you didn't miss it.

CHEVROLET WTCC ULTRA (2006)

At the 2006 Paris auto salon there were some great new concepts, while breathtaking production cars were being unveiled all over the place. So for Chevrolet to proclaim that its WTCC Ultra concept was the 'star of the show' was just a little bit optimistic, to say the least. Here was a car that took all the usual touring car clichés and stuck them onto a humdrum Chevrolet saloon (sedan) – although, to be fair, it did look pretty sensational by the time junior designer Ewan Kingsbury had worked some magic. But while the WTCC Ultra made Chevrolet look good (albeit only briefly), this was not a concept that introduced anything genuinely fresh to the automotive world.

SPECIFICATION

ORIGIN	Asia/Europe/USA
DEBUT	Paris 2006
ENGINE CAPACITY	1991cc (121cu in) turbocharged
CONFIGURATION	Front-mounted diesel four-cylinder
TRANSMISSION	Five-speed manual, rear-wheel drive
POWER	142kW (190bhp)
TOP SPEED	N/A
LENGTH	4324mm (170in)
WIDTH	1906mm (75in)

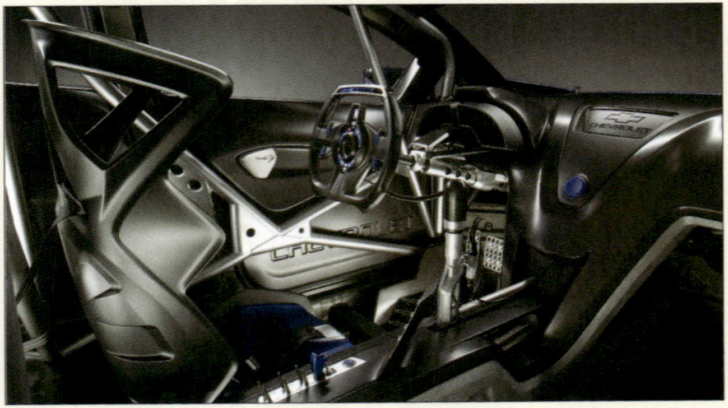

Left: *The WTCC Ultra's single-seat interior was classic touring car, with lots of bare alloy, no soundproofing and exposed linkages for everything.*

There was no high-revving, ultra-peaky petrol (gasoline) engine under the bonnet (hood); instead there was a 142kW (190bhp) turbodiesel.

The design work was carried out in South Korea, Switzerland, the United States and Australia; final construction took place in Japan.

The bodykit was constructed of fibreglass and carbon-fibre, in a bid to keep the weight down as much as possible.

It looks like a boy racer's dream, but those skirts, spoilers, scoops and slats all work to keep the WTCC Ultra cool and stuck to the road.

CHEVROLET NOMAD (1999)

This was not the first Chevrolet Nomad concept – and it also was not the last. The original had debuted in 1954 and it would lead to the fabulous Tri-Chevy Nomad of the following year. This edition would not lead to any production car – thank goodness – and neither would the third Nomad concept of 2004. Whereas the earlier Nomad concept and production cars were well proportioned, stylish and completely desirable, the 1999 edition was badly proportioned, bland and an utter disappointment after what had gone before. Still, at least Chevrolet redeemed itself with an identically named concept five years later – even if it led nowhere.

SPECIFICATION

ORIGIN	USA
DEBUT	Detroit 1999
ENGINE CAPACITY	N/A
CONFIGURATION	Front-mounted V8
TRANSMISSION	Automatic, rear-wheel drive
POWER	N/A
TOP SPEED	N/A
LENGTH	N/A
WIDTH	N/A

Left: *Helping to increase practicality, the tailgate slid into the bodywork to aid loading, plus the front seat slid away to increase interior capacity.*

The rear of the roof featured a 36-slat venetian blind, which allowed the Nomad's interior to be opened up to the elements.

There were three rows of seats to turn this into a people-carrier; the middle and back row could be folded flat into the floor.

Although there was just the one door on the passenger side, the driver's side featured an extra door, which slid back.

A Chevrolet small-block V8 was installed in the nose, but GM did not offer any displacement or power figures.

CHRYSLER IMPERIAL *(2006)*

Imitation may be the sincerest form of flattery, but it is hard to see Rolls-Royce feeling too good about themselves when the wraps were taken off Chrysler's Imperial. Looking like a mildly restyled Rolls Phantom – with the emphasis being on mildly – the Imperial's profile and detailing borrowed heavily from the rather more prestigious Brit, from its 56cm (22in) wheels to its suicide rear doors. All that was missing were the waterfall grille and spirit of ecstasy – which no doubt Chrysler's designers would have fitted if they had only had just a little bit more time to get the concept ready …

SPECIFICATION

ORIGIN	USA
DEBUT	Detroit 2006
ENGINE CAPACITY	5.7 litres (348cu in)
CONFIGURATION	Front-mounted V8
TRANSMISSION	Five-speed auto, rear-wheel drive
POWER	254kW (340bhp)
TOP SPEED	257km/h (160mph)
LENGTH	5439mm (214in)
WIDTH	1933mm (76in)

Left: ***A very Seventies colour scheme was chosen, with brown paintwork outside and tan/magnolia hide for the cabin – with lashings of timber too.***

The lighting was bang up to date, with LEDs up front for everything except the headlights, and circles of LEDs at the back.

The Imperial's most important characteristic was its stately demeanour; passengers sat 18cm (seven inches) higher than in a Chrysler 300C, for example.

There was masses of LED lighting inside as well, with overhead cabin lighting and instrument backlighting provided by LEDs.

The Imperial's wheelbase was stretched to 3124mm (123in), but this still was not enough to give the right proportions; it looked too squashed.

DAEWOO NO.1 *(1994)*

Check out those pictures, then try to claim the words 'silk purse' and 'sow's ear' do not spring to mind. If you take a truly bad car and lop the roof off, you're not going to end up with anything even remotely desirable, so Daewoo was wasting its time when it took its Lanos hatch and turned it into a droptop. Daewoo was clearly having a bit of a joke when it created the No.1 – then decided to have another when it had to come up with a name. The Korean company clearly realized that No One would buy one of the things, so it named the car appropriately.

SPECIFICATION

ORIGIN	Korea
DEBUT	Birmingham 1994
ENGINE CAPACITY	1.6 litres (98cu in)
CONFIGURATION	Front-mounted four-cylinder
TRANSMISSION	Five-speed manual, front-wheel drive
POWER	82kW (110bhp)
TOP SPEED	N/A
LENGTH	4240mm (167in)
WIDTH	1680mm (66in)

Left: ***Daewoo could not get enough of the No.1, which is why the car was tweaked, then shown at the 1995 Seoul motor show – and the Frankfurt event too.***

The No.1 was created by Daewoo's British technical centre, which is why the car was unveiled at the 1994 British motor show.

As the base car was the production Lanos, the No.1 could be put into production easily – which Daewoo attempted to do. But failed.

The original No.1 was a two-seater, but became a 2+2. It was also retrimmed inside, gaining leather and alloy details in the process.

There was no folding hardtop here; instead there was an electrically operated fabric roof which stowed flush behind the back seat.

DODGE CIRCUIT EV (2009)

As part of the Chrysler Group, Dodge was on the verge of bankruptcy early in 2009. In a bid to secure government handouts it was forced to commit to producing more energy-efficient cars, such as those propelled by hybrid powertrains and electric motors. Little development time meant that Chrysler had to resort to shortcuts – which basically entailed taking a few of its production cars and sticking a badge on the side, proclaiming them to be EVs, or electric vehicles. But Dodge did not have anything especially exciting in its line-up, so it plundered Lotus's range and stuck an EV badge on the English company's Europa. Result: an energy-efficient sportscar. How exciting.

SPECIFICATION

ORIGIN	USA
DEBUT	Detroit 2009
ENGINE CAPACITY	Electric vehicle
CONFIGURATION	Mid-mounted electric motor
TRANSMISSION	N/A
POWER	200kW (268bhp)
TOP SPEED	In excess of 195km/h (120mph)
LENGTH	3900mm (154in)
WIDTH	1714mm (67in)

Left: *With a lithium-ion battery, the EV could manage 240–320km (150–200 miles) between charges; it could be topped up from a domestic electricity supply.*

Despite its eco credentials, the EV was packed with kit such as leather trim, air conditioning, powered windows and a premium sound system.

The bodywork was finished in 'Tangoreen' paintwork, while there was a huge 'EV' decal running along each flank.

Thanks to torque aplenty from the electric motor, the EV could cover the 0–100km/h (0–60mph) sprint in under five seconds.

Although the Circuit was clearly based on the Evora, Dodge updated it with a revised nose, fresh tail and some great new alloys.

FIAT TREPIUNO (2004)

If you are really struggling as a car maker, but you have something special in your past, the answer invariably seems to be to plunder your heritage shamelessly. That's exactly what Fiat did, rolling out the Trepiuno, which was nothing more than a 1950s 500 for the twenty-first century. Still it worked for BMW with the Mini and VW with the Beetle, so why shouldn't this ailing Italian company try the same trick? It's a trick that worked too, as Fiat put the Trepiuno into production and the car went down a storm – proving that you do not have to look forwards to be successful.

SPECIFICATION

ORIGIN	Italy
DEBUT	Geneva 2004
ENGINE CAPACITY	N/A
CONFIGURATION	Front-mounted
TRANSMISSION	Front-wheel drive
POWER	N/A
TOP SPEED	N/A
LENGTH	3300mm (130in)
WIDTH	N/A

Left: *The Trepiuno took its name from the Italian for 'three plus one' – it was capable of seating three comfortably, and an extra one on short journeys.*

Whereas the original 500 featured a sliding cloth sunroof to open up the cabin to the elements, here there was a fixed-glass panel.

Unlike the original 500, this new edition featured an engine mounted in the nose of the car, rather than the rear.

Fiat clearly got the Trepiuno's design right; it was barely altered in the transition to production car, and the 500 proved a smash hit.

At no point did Fiat make any references to the Trepiuno's running gear, suggesting the concept was a non-runner.

FORD FORTY-NINE (2001)

The all-new Fords for 1949 looked fantastic – the Forty-Nine concept of just over half a century later did not. Looking more like a lead sled from the hot-rod scene, the Forty-Nine was penned by J Mays – who had also been guilty of the VW Concept 1 which became the New Beetle, proving that he felt no guilt in nicking old designs and dressing them up as something supposedly new. For 2001 there was a Forty-Nine coupé, and the following year a convertible was rolled out, neither of which really took much from their 1950s predecessors. Thankfully, unlike the equally creatively bankrupt Ford Thunderbird concept of 1998, the Forty-Nine did not see production.

SPECIFICATION	
ORIGIN	USA
DEBUT	Detroit 2001
ENGINE CAPACITY	3934cc (240cu in)
CONFIGURATION	Front-mounted V8
TRANSMISSION	Five-speed manual, rear-wheel drive
POWER	N/A
TOP SPEED	N/A
LENGTH	N/A
WIDTH	N/A

Left: ***A cantilevered bench-style front seat was power-actuated, while a floating centre console ran the length of the interior.***

Ford hoped that the Forty-Nine concept would be as successful a production car as the original, which notched up 1.3 million pre-orders.

The car's hyper-smooth appearance was achieved by an all-glass upper body structure with concealed pillars and windscreen wipers.

There was high-intensity discharge (HID) and projector-beam front lighting; at the rear there were wraparound LED lights.

The audio system featured a multidisc CD changer and a massive sub-woofer, driven by a 200-watt amplifier.

FORD ELTEC (1985)

The fact that the Mk5 Escort went down in history as one of the least-capable family cars ever does not make the Eltec look better with the passing of time; this concept offered a glimpse of what Ford's fifth take on the Escort would look like. The name was an abbreviation of ELectronic TEChnology, on account of the computerization of various systems such as the anti-lock brakes, traction control and high-intensity headlights. The engine's functions, as well as the air suspension, were also controlled by computer – so it is a great shame that the designers did not give the Eltec a more daring set of clothes to wear.

SPECIFICATION

ORIGIN	Germany/UK
DEBUT	Frankfurt 1985
ENGINE CAPACITY	1.3 litres (79cu in)
CONFIGURATION	Front-mounted four-cylinder
TRANSMISSION	Continuously variable transmission, front-wheel drive
POWER	60kW (80bhp)
TOP SPEED	N/A
LENGTH	N/A
WIDTH	N/A

Left: ***The Eltec featured an unusual amount of glass – which meant that there was superb all-round visibility – while the roof was also largely constructed of glass.***

The Eltec was a thinly disguised foretaste of the Mk5 Escort – the nose, profile and rear were all much the same.

Details such as high-mounted rear lights were deemed too radical for production, although they were to become increasingly popular.

Active ride meant that the Eltec's suspension was controlled by computer for composed cornering, while also offering a comfortable ride.

The 1.3-litre (79cu in) lean-burn petrol (gasoline) engine offered adequate power, while also being kind to the environment.

HOLDEN EFIJY *(2005)*

Now this really was lazy design. Take one 1950s FJ model and customize it heavily, adding masses of ultra-modern technology to come up with a feel-good concept. The thing was, this could have been plucked straight from a custom car show, which is really where it belonged. After all, concepts are about looking forwards – not back. And the Efijy merely re-created the golden era of Holden, while quietly attempting to dismiss its twenty-first century woes. At least the Efijy looked good – but it did not offer anything new for Holden's production cars, which is why the concept made just one major motor show appearance, then was quietly forgotten.

SPECIFICATION

ORIGIN	Australia
DEBUT	Sydney 2005
ENGINE CAPACITY	6 litres (366cu in) supercharged
CONFIGURATION	Front-mounted V8
TRANSMISSION	Four-speed auto, rear-wheel drive
POWER	481kw (645bhp)
TOP SPEED	N/A
LENGTH	5162mm (203in)
WIDTH	1999mm (79in)

Left: ***When the Efijy was being driven its ground clearance was 139mm (5½in), but for show it could be dropped to within just 27mm (1in) from the ground.***

The wheels were aluminium alloy; they measured 508 x 229mm (20 x 9in) at the front and 559 x 254mm (22 x 10in) at the rear, with 35 and 30-profile tyres respectively.

Most of the Efijy's interior and exterior lighting was by LED, including the headlights, taillights, indicators and brake lights.

The 6-litre (366cu in) V8 was borrowed from the Corvette, and supercharged to produce a very healthy 481kW (645bhp).

Pulling the car up were 381mm (15in) ventilated disc brakes with six-pot callipers at the front and four-pot items at the rear.

HONDA J-MW (1997)

When it comes to the bare minimum of effort, Honda should win an award for this creation, so close was it to a production car. Those people who have gone to the accessories shop, then spent a couple of weekends applying decals and installing a fresh stereo could be accused of having put in more effort than Honda's designers. This was one of four concepts unveiled at the 1997 Tokyo motor show, all with a 'J' in the name to denote 'joyful' – as in a joyful ownership and driving experience. Whether owners really would have derived a particularly joyful experience of any kind in this is highly questionable.

SPECIFICATION

ORIGIN	Japan
DEBUT	Tokyo 1997
ENGINE CAPACITY	1.5 litres (92cu in)
CONFIGURATION	Front-mounted four-cylinder
TRANSMISSION	Continuously variable transmission, four-wheel drive
POWER	N/A
TOP SPEED	N/A
LENGTH	3710mm (146in)
WIDTH	1695mm (67in)

Left: ***The J-MW's name was an abbreviation of Multi-Joyful Hobby Car (!), to reflect its supposedly multifaceted nature.***

2Practicality was the key here, with a flexible interior layout, and a flat floor to free up as much space as possible.

There was plenty of kit fitted, such as dual sunroofs, air conditioning, a laptop computer and a high-end stereo – but it was hardly high-tech.

The J-MW's compact dimensions ensured that it was suitable for whizzing around town, where it would prove agile and easy to park.

In a further attempt to make it easier to live with urban traffic, there was a continuously variable transmission fitted.

HUMMER H3T *(2004)*

A really good concept can come close to reinventing the wheel, packing in fresh technologies and really moving the game on. Then there are concepts such as the Hummer H3T, which takes an existing product, tweaks it and makes so little difference to the automotive landscape that nobody notices. Indeed, all the H3T did was take the existing 'small' Hummer SUV and turn it into a pick-up – hardly anything to make a song and dance about. Of course, that's exactly what Hummer did, claiming its new 'baby' was revolutionary – even though it would be in production within a year.

SPECIFICATION

ORIGIN	USA
DEBUT	Los Angeles 2004
ENGINE CAPACITY	3464cc (211cu in) turbocharged
CONFIGURATION	Front-mounted five-cylinder
TRANSMISSION	Four-speed auto, four-wheel drive
POWER	261kW (350bhp)
TOP SPEED	N/A
LENGTH	4443mm (175in)
WIDTH	1893mm (75in)

Left: *The H3T's cabin and its exterior were both littered with solid aluminium details such as the dash inserts and door handles.*

Mechanicals carried over direct from the regular H3 meant a 3.5-litre (211cu in) five-cylinder engine, turbocharged to give 261kW (350bhp) and 475Nm (350lbf ft) of torque.

All of the exterior lighting was via light-emitting diodes, which were ultra-modern, compact and efficient, as well as durable.

When Hummer turned the concept into a production car, it became a double cab with a short bed – not nearly as useful.

As with all Hummers, this was not just for show; it could perform too. Ground clearance was 292mm (11½in) and it could climb mountains.

JAGUAR XK180 *(1998)*

You could not deny that the XK180 looked truly fabulous from every angle. Utterly gorgeous and a car that would have been sought after from the day of its announcement had it gone into production. But it was still little more than an XK Speedster; a regular XK convertible with a heavily revised glasshouse and some fairings. It also drew rather too heavily on the D-Type racer of the 1950s, even though it was released to mark the fiftieth anniversary of the iconic XK120. In short, the XK180 offered nothing that looked to the future – every single element was a nod to the past.

SPECIFICATION

ORIGIN	GB
DEBUT	Paris 1998
ENGINE CAPACITY	3996cc (244cu in) supercharged
CONFIGURATION	Front-mounted V8
TRANSMISSION	Five-speed auto, rear-wheel drive
POWER	336kW (450bhp)
TOP SPEED	290km/h (180mph)
LENGTH	N/A
WIDTH	N/A

Left: *Jaguar's engineers overhauled the AJ-V8 engine to produce a very healthy 336kW (450bhp), to give a projected speed of 290km/h (180mph).*

A five-speed automatic transmission was fitted, with ratios selectable via steering wheel-mounted buttons.

The bodyshell was hand-beaten aluminium for lightness, while the interior featured swathes of engine-turned alloy and leather trim.

Valeo developed a special rear light cluster, which contained 24 light-emitting diodes for the brake, tail and indicator lights.

One of the biggest tasks in creating the XK180 was to reduce the wheelbase by 127mm (five inches), to maintain proportions.

JEEP VARSITY (2000)

Jeep set out to create a fresh vehicle sector with its Varsity – as if there were not already enough from which to choose. The problem for Jeep was that the ugly SUV was already available elsewhere, so this did not really break new ground. Bizarrely, Jeep claimed that this was the 'go-anywhere do-anything urban adventure concept' – so it was designed for trail blazers who liked to get off the beaten track … as long as that was in town. With such a mixed brief, it is no wonder that the Varsity suffered from an identitiy crisis; thankfully those styling cues were quickly forgotten.

SPECIFICATION

ORIGIN	USA
DEBUT	Detroit 2000
ENGINE CAPACITY	3.5 litres (214cu in)
CONFIGURATION	Front-mounted V6
TRANSMISSION	Automatic, four-wheel drive
POWER	224kW (300bhp)
TOP SPEED	210km/h (130mph)
LENGTH	4224mm (166in)
WIDTH	1770mm (70in)

Left: *Although this was an SUV for the urban environment, there was still four-wheel drive, complete with high and low range.*

Onlookers were left in no doubt as to who made the Varsity, with that prominent seven-slat grille and the Jeep wording below.

You might think that only a V8 would do in an American car of this size, but instead there was a 3.5-litre (214cu in) V6 engine.

The interior was made of heavy-duty materials, with the design of most major components inspired by pieces of outdoor equipment.

To give the car a sporty stance there were 483mm (19in) wheels at each corner, each one wrapped in a 235/55R tyre.

LAMBORGHINI MIURA *(2006)*

Ask a hundred car nuts to name the most beautiful cars ever created, and the original Lamborghini Miura would be guaranteed to score highly – probably in the top three. As a result, with the original production Miura looking sensational, this concept was guaranteed to do the same – because it was a direct copy, albeit subtly updated. It may have looked fantastic, but it committed the cardinal sin of looking towards the past rather than ahead to the future, which is one of the laziest forms of design. As a result, there is no way that Lamborghini, a firm renowned for its cutting-edge designs, could put this concept into production.

SPECIFICATION

ORIGIN	Italy
DEBUT	Detroit 2006
ENGINE CAPACITY	Non-runner
CONFIGURATION	Mid-engined
TRANSMISSION	Probably six-speed sequential, four-wheel drive
POWER	In excess of 373kW (500bhp)
TOP SPEED	In excess of 320km/h (200mph)
LENGTH	N/A
WIDTH	N/A

Left: *This concept did not run; Lamborghini did not talk about what the running gear might have been, but it would have had to be a V12 engine.*

The Miura concept was wheeled out in 2006 – four decades after the original Miura had made its debut at the Geneva motor show.

By the time this concept debuted, Lamborghini was committed to four-wheel drive for its cars, so no doubt the Miura would have featured it.

One of the most distinctive elements of the original Miura's design was the flip-up headlight design. The reincarnation featured faired-in units instead.

The original Miura had been fitted with Campagnolo alloy wheels; these were not a direct copy, but did feature elements of the design.

MERCURY COUGAR S (1999)

Some of the other concepts in this chapter have one thing in their favour; they offered a preview of a production car. Not this one, though; Mercury waited until its Cougar had entered production, then spent all of an hour coming up with this 'concept', which was little more than a styling kit on a standard car. Created by Ford's Special Vehicle Engineering division, the Cougar S was followed up by the equally unexciting Eliminator. This featured suspension set five centimetres (two inches) lower and a quartet of tail pipes, plus some meatier wheels and a styling kit. There were upgraded mechanicals, too, but this was hardly innovative stuff.

SPECIFICATION

ORIGIN	USA
DEBUT	Detroit 1999
ENGINE CAPACITY	3 litres (183cu in)
CONFIGURATION	Front-mounted four-cylinder
TRANSMISSION	Five-speed manual, four-wheel drive
POWER	160kW (215bhp)
TOP SPEED	N/A
LENGTH	4700mm (185in)
WIDTH	1770mm (70in)

Left: *While the production Cougar featured drive to the front wheels only, this concept was fitted with four-wheel drive.*

Styling extras included a functional bonnet (hood) scoop and a pair of spoilers for the rear, plus deep-dish 457mm (18in) alloy wheels.

The interior was carried over largely unchanged, but there were Recaro racing seats for those in the front, plus alloy pedals.

The most obvious difference between the Cougar S and production editions was the styling kit, featuring flared wheelarches.

There was a revised nose, incorporating integrated fog lights and a mesh grille to aid engine cooling.

NISSAN TRAILRUNNER *(1997)*

Welcome to the world of excess youthful testosterone and unformed (or should that be malformed?) tastes. Clad with a rear wing (fender) the size of a wallpaperer's pasting table and three-spoke alloys straight out of the bargain-basement mail-order catalogue, the Trailrunner was a boy racer's dream, offering zero style but lines that were eye-catching for all the wrong reasons. Nissan clearly realized its mistake because it never pursued these themes for its production cars, but flirting with them on a concept was no excuse – and still a major error of judgment.

SPECIFICATION

ORIGIN	Japan
DEBUT	Frankfurt 1997
ENGINE CAPACITY	2 litres (122cu in)
CONFIGURATION	Front-mounted four-cylinder
TRANSMISSION	Six-speed manual, four-wheel drive
POWER	142kW (190bhp)
TOP SPEED	N/A
LENGTH	4230mm (167in)
WIDTH	1760mm (69in)

Left: *The interior looked a good deal better than its exterior, with a black-and-yellow colour scheme (for those who like primary colours) and plenty of high-tech equipment.*

Practicality was not considered too important because the car was aimed at young drivers – hence the coupé configuration.

That rear spoiler had to be as large as it was because it was an extension of the roof when a rack needed to be fitted.

Those nasty three-spoke alloy wheels measured 457mm (18in) across. The spare was accessed via a slide-out tray in the rear panel.

All four wheels were driven via a six-speed manual gearbox. Power was provided by a 2-litre (122cu in) petrol (gasoline) engine.

NISSAN STYLISH6 *(1997)*

This car deserves to be included in the worst concepts of all time just for its name – how long did it take for Nissan's marketing team to come up with 'Stylish6'? And was a concept car ever named less appropriately? Boxy, bland and unexciting in every way, the Stylish6 was capable of carrying six people – but not in anything approaching style. Still, at least there was a certain degree of comfort on offer, thanks to a cabin that offered plenty of equipment and space. This would also prove to be much closer to production cars of the early twenty-first century than many other contemporary concepts.

SPECIFICATION

ORIGIN	Japan
DEBUT	Tokyo 1997
ENGINE CAPACITY	2.5 litres (153cu in)
CONFIGURATION	Front-mounted V6 plus electric motor
TRANSMISSION	CVT, front-wheel drive
POWER	N/A
TOP SPEED	N/A
LENGTH	4800mm (189in)
WIDTH	1780mm (70in)

Left: ***In the Stylish6 the front two rows of passengers got their own individual seats; those in the back had to make do with a folding bench seat.***

Power was supplied by a hybrid powertrain, in which a petrol (gasoline) engine was assisted by an electric motor, driven via a continuously variable transmission.

The Stylish6's cabin was trimmed in light materials; to open it up further there was also a roof made of green-tinted glass.

The cabin was also stuffed with gadgets such as a head-up display and an 18cm (seven-inch) liquid crystal display in the central console.

The six occupants were carried in three rows of two, which was surely the least efficient way of carrying passengers.

PONTIAC GTO *(1999)*

If ever there was an example of truly cynical marketing, this was it. One of the all-time great American automotive brands was the original Pontiac GTO of the late 1960s – and this concept simply took the name and debased it. It was telling that, in the GTO's press kit, Pontiac devoted much more space to the original muscle car than to the new concept; there was rather more glory in the former. Instead of pursuing the design themes in the GTO, Pontiac would go on to produce one lame duck after another – so it was no surprise when a decade after the arrival of the GTO concept, it was announced that Pontiac would be closing its doors for good.

SPECIFICATION

ORIGIN	USA
DEBUT	Detroit 1999
ENGINE CAPACITY	Non-runner
CONFIGURATION	Front-mounted V8
TRANSMISSION	Rear-wheel drive
POWER	N/A
TOP SPEED	N/A
LENGTH	N/A
WIDTH	N/A

Left: *Perhaps the best thing about this concept was the colour used on the outside; the distinctive orange paintwork harked back to the original GTO.*

There was aggression everywhere, from the prominent nose and narrow headlights to the vents in the A-pillar.

Several design cues were carried over from the original GTO, such as the bonnet (hood) scoops, split grille and raised haunches at the rear.

The glasshouse was very narrow, while the waistline was rather high, looking almost as if the GTO had been subjected to a roof chop.

The specially designed wheels were 483mm (19in) items at the front, while those at the back measured an extra 25mm (one inch) across.

RENAULT FIFTIE *(1996)*

The name said it all: this was a concept built to celebrate half a century of Renault's brilliant post-war people's car, the 4CV. That was a vehicle that truly put the nation on wheels, but the Fiftie was to the 4CV what Volkswagen's Concept 1 was to the original Beetle. Renault realized that the Fiftie was fundamentally flawed because of this – it was rear-engined, like its predecessor, resulting in awful packaging. At least VW had the good sense to move the engine to the front, rather than slavishly follow its original car's layout. The Fiftie, meanwhile, was never capable of consideration for production because Renault would have needed to start again to make it viable.

SPECIFICATION

ORIGIN	France
DEBUT	Geneva 1996
ENGINE CAPACITY	1149cc (70cu in)
CONFIGURATION	Rear-mounted in-line four
TRANSMISSION	Five-speed semi-auto, rear-wheel drive
POWER	45kW (60bhp)
TOP SPEED	N/A
LENGTH	N/A
WIDTH	N/A

Left: *The Fiftie's interior featured natual materials such as rattan, cotton and linen, to give a back-to-basics feel. Aluminium detailing brought things up to date.*

Aluminium detailing on the outside helped to lift the car's lines while also giving it a contemporary look.

The car's lines were based on those of the 4CV of the post-war period, but the packaging was compromised because of the mechanical layout.

The roof featured a series of slats, to open up the interior. The cabin could be opened up even further by folding the rear window flat.

Like the car that inspired it, the Fiftie was rear-engined, thanks to its Sport Spider platform – although the engine was merely a 1149cc (70cu in) unit.

TOYOTA XYR (1999)

Oh dear – does anything really need to be said here? Just a quick glance at the pictures shows what a lame excuse for a concept the XYR was. Take one Celica pre-production coupé and stick on the biggest rear spoiler you can find at the local accessories shop – then roll it out as a 'high-performance sports coupé concept' and you have one of the least imaginative concept cars ever. Perhaps Toyota's plan was to shock everyone with the tastelessness of that rear wing (fender), so that when the production car was brought out from under wraps a few months later there would be sighs of relief all round that the company had introduced a new sportscar that exhibited such restrained styling.

SPECIFICATION

ORIGIN	Japan
DEBUT	Detroit 1999
ENGINE CAPACITY	1795cc (110cu in)
CONFIGURATION	Front-mounted four-cylinder
TRANSMISSION	Four-speed auto, front-wheel drive
POWER	134kW (180bhp)
TOP SPEED	225km/h (140mph)
LENGTH	4333mm (171in)
WIDTH	1737mm (68in)

Left: *Under the bonnet (hood) of the XYR was an all-new aluminium alloy twin-cam engine, capable of pushing out 134kW (180bhp), thanks to variable valve timing.*

Take that rear wing (fender) away, tidy up the lower portion of the nose and you have Toyota's seventh-generation Celica.

To make the most of the available power, Toyota kept weight to a minimum; the XYR tipped the scales at just 1140kg (2513lb).

The XYR was designed to appeal to young buyers, which is why the interior featured bucket seats and race-style instrumentation.

The alloy wheels played their part in making the XYR look desirable; they were 432mm (17in) across and masked disc brakes all round.

VOLKSWAGEN CONCEPT 1 (1994)

With more than 20 million of the original model already built, did the world really need a production run of several more million Beetles? VW clearly thought so, when it rebodied its Golf to create a Beetle for the twenty-first century. Offering less practicality than the Golf that sired it, the new-generation Beetle was also more costly – but that didn't stop buyers queuing up for one when the model first went on sale. By the time the production hatchback arrived, Volkswagen had also shown a convertible edition of the Concept 1 – this would also go into production soon after the arrival of the hatch.

SPECIFICATION

ORIGIN	Germany
DEBUT	Detroit 1994
ENGINE CAPACITY	1896cc (116cu in) turbocharged
CONFIGURATION	Front-mounted in-line four-cylinder diesel
TRANSMISSION	Five-speed auto
POWER	82kW (110bhp)
TOP SPEED	179km/h (111mph)
LENGTH	3824mm (151in)
WIDTH	1633mm (64in)

Left: *In the 1990s, heritage and retro designs were everywhere, and Volkswagen was very quick to cash in on the fact that it made the bestselling car ever.*

The design roots of the Concept 1 were obvious, but the mechanical configuration was completely different, and it worked.

Under all those curves was a water-cooled engine, mounted at the front – the first concept was a non-runner. There was also front-wheel drive.

The Concept 1 sat on narrow 457mm (18in) wheels. By the time that the car reached production, much smaller wheels would be fitted.

The equipment count was high, but the interior design was understated. Air bags, air conditioning and a stereo had to be housed, but it was all retro.

VOLKSWAGEN RAGSTER (2005)

As if a rehashed version of an old car was not enough, Volkswagen took its New Beetle in 2005 and did a Porsche with it by creating a Speedster edition. Credit where it is due, the Ragster looked good, but it was not innovative in any way as it applied decades-old styling themes. Even the car's name was an amalgam of old terminologies; it mixed ragtop with speedster with the result being horribly contrived. The relative lack of effort on the bodywork and interior was not the only shortcoming. VW did not even bother to make the car a runner because there was no engine fitted at all. Clearly its maker didn't have much faith in the project …

SPECIFICATION

ORIGIN	Germany
DEBUT	Detroit 2005
ENGINE CAPACITY	N/A
CONFIGURATION	Front-mounted
TRANSMISSION	Front-wheel drive
POWER	N/A
TOP SPEED	N/A
LENGTH	4081mm (161in)
WIDTH	1724mm (68in)

Left: *In the transition from Beetle to Ragster, the interior received an overhaul, with race-style bucket seats and steering wheel with integral start button.*

Styling was beefed up over the regular Beetle, with extended wings (fenders) and bumpers, plus upgraded Brembo brakes.

Roof chops are a classic hot-rod styling cue; the Ragster's roof was lowered by 150mm (six inches) compared with a standard Beetle.

VW did not specify what engine would be fitted to the Ragster; it claimed petrol (gasoline) and diesel engines were both suited to the car.

Those bespoke aluminium alloy wheels measured 483mm (19in) across and were wrapped in 235/60 R19 tyres.

VOLVO PERFORMANCE CONCEPT CAR 2 (2001)

If you are coming up with a performance-car concept, high on the wish list would be a rakish two-seater body, a mid-mounted multi-cylinder engine, and looks to die for. Or, if you are Volvo, you could just take your largest family estate (station wagon), bolt on some alloy wheels and call it your new concept. Which is just what the Swedish company did with its imaginatively named Performance Car Concept 2, based on the V70 and looking like a decently rakish brick. This was the sequel to the Performance Car Concept, based on the S60 saloon (sedan) and looking not much more inspired.

SPECIFICATION

ORIGIN	Sweden
DEBUT	Frankfurt 2001
ENGINE CAPACITY	2435cc (149cu in) turbocharged
CONFIGURATION	Front-mounted five-cylinder
TRANSMISSION	Six-speed manual, four-wheel drive
POWER	224kW (300bhp)
TOP SPEED	250km/h (155mph)
LENGTH	4710mm (185in)
WIDTH	1800mm (71in)

Left: *Helping to pull all the power down was a four-wheel drive transmission, while the gearbox was a six-speed manual.*

The PCC 2 previewed Volvo's V70R, with a specification that was virtually identical to the concept – although the production car was more understated.

Volvo's trusty 2.4-litre (149cu in) engine was in the nose of the PCC 2, turbocharged to produce a very fruity 224kW (300bhp).

Sharp looks were key to the PCC 2, which is why there were 483mm (19in) BBS alloy wheels fitted, shod with 245/35 tyres.

Styling cues introduced on the PCC 2 included the aluminium-finished front air dam and side skirts, plus an alloy grille.

COMPLETELY POINTLESS

Designers live in a fantasy world; they are well known for it and a bit of escapism never hurt anyone, did it? Well, no – but while these pointless machines were being dreamed up, their designers could have been solving genuine problems with real-world cars that left the world a better place. For example, did we really need a car that incorporated its own mixing desk? Or a vehicle that featured a hovercraft deck at the back?

Not all pointless concepts are quite so extreme though – some don't even serve as fun show cars because they don't push the boundaries in any particular way. Take the Italdesign Formula 4 – a four-seater barchetta, which kind of defeats the object – or the Castagna Crossup, a pick-up with the world's smallest load bay. These then are the concepts which came with a brief that was a complete waste of time; those for which there would be no buyers no matter how sleek the design or how cutting-edge the technology they packed. They really were completely pointless.

Left: ***The Jeep Treo is possibly the least useful concept ever devised; poor ground clearance and a tiny cabin were only two of its many faults.***

AUDI AL2 OPEN END (1997)

When Audi unveiled its AL2 at the 1997 Frankfurt motor show, it was clear that the car would go into production – which it did as the ill-fated A2. When the Open End edition was unwrapped a month later, however, everybody wondered why on Earth Audi had bothered – the car was nothing short of pointless. Audi claimed the Open End was 'relaxed and unconstrained, carefree, rough-taking and nimble. It literally holds its head high, always taking the right approach to life.' Er, right – so it's a complete waste of space, then, justified by Audi with a series of random words.

SPECIFICATION

ORIGIN	Germany
DEBUT	Tokyo 1997
ENGINE CAPACITY	1390cc (85cu in)
CONFIGURATION	Front-mounted in-line four
TRANSMISSION	Five-speed manual, front-wheel drive
POWER	75kW (100bhp)
TOP SPEED	192km/h (119mph)
LENGTH	3765mm (148in)
WIDTH	1620mm (64in)

Left: *The AL2 Open End's tailgate could be retracted electrically by remote control, slotting down into the rear fender where it disappeared from view.*

The engine, taken from Volkswagen's Polo, was a 1.4-litre (85cu in) petrol (gasoline) unit. With a weight of just 790kg (1742lb), the Open End had decent performance.

Audi is one of the few car makers that has championed the aluminium monocoque; the AL2's bodyshell was constructed of light alloy.

Safety was a key feature of the Open End, with six airbags installed, plus high-tech lights, anti-lock brakes and electronic brake force distribution.

To maintain stiffness and also safety in the event of the car rolling over, those side rails remained fixed.

AUDI STEPPENWOLF (2000)

How many market segments do you need to combine in order to come up with a successful car? Plenty if you take into account Audi's Steppenwolf, which mixed an SUV with a coupé and convertible, with a bit of family hatch and even some luxury limo thrown in for good measure. The idea behind the Steppenwolf was that it could go off-roading while carrying four people in complete comfort – although the seriously ill-proportioned three-door configuration would not have been too appealing to the well-heeled buyers at whom this concept was aimed. Unsurprisingly, this was one concept that Audi did not see through to production.

SPECIFICATION

ORIGIN	Germany
DEBUT	Paris 2000
ENGINE CAPACITY	3189cc (195cu in)
CONFIGURATION	Front-mounted V6
TRANSMISSION	Six-speed manual, four-wheel drive
POWER	168kW (225bhp)
TOP SPEED	233km/h (145mph)
LENGTH	N/A
WIDTH	N/A

Left: *To enable the Steppenwolf to do some true off-roading, there was height-adjustable air suspension, offering up to 223mm (8¾in) of ground clearance.*

The main problem with the styling was the length behind the side doors; the Steppenwolf looked as if it had been stretched.

The roof was made of carbon-fibre and it was detachable; it could be replaced with a soft-top that stretched over the open roof.

As you would expect of a high-end Audi, there was quattro four-wheel drive to ensure the power could be put down whatever the conditions.

The 3.2-litre (195cu in) V6 engine ensured strong performance; the 0–100km/h (0–62mph) sprint could be dispatched in under eight seconds.

BERTONE SLIM (2000)

When it comes to automotive culs-de-sac, few could have come to a dead end quite as swiftly as this one, a two-seater city car that was ridiculously flawed. It may have offered better crash safety and weather protection than the motorbike it was claimed to beat, but the Slim also featured four wheels, so it required a car licence to drive in the UK – although in Europe such 'quadricycles' could be driven by 14-year-olds. In essence the Slim was a Messerschmitt bubble-car-style microcar for the twenty-first century – except that it was longer than a Mini, if rather more narrow.

SPECIFICATION

ORIGIN	Italy
DEBUT	Geneva 2000
ENGINE CAPACITY	505cc (31cu in)
CONFIGURATION	Rear-mounted two-cylinder
TRANSMISSION	CVT, rear-wheel drive
POWER	15kW (20bhp)
TOP SPEED	120km/h (75mph)
LENGTH	3200mm (126in)
WIDTH	1100mm (43in)

Left: *Two versions of the Slim were proposed: one with two-cylinder petrol (gasoline) power and the other with a 10kW (13bhp) electric motor.*

The two occupants sat in tandem, making conversation tricky. The narrow track also would not have helped stability.

Each occupant got their own canopy, which slid back for entry and exit. The roof was made of tinted glass.

There were doors on one side only, to prevent occupants stepping out into traffic. Unless the car was driven in countries which drove on the left …

There was a disc brake at each corner, with 381mm (15in) alloy wheels being fitted to keep the car's weight down.

CASTAGNA CROSSUP (2005)

If you exercise some subtlety and restraint, it is often possible to improve on an already good-looking car. If you don't have a clue what you're doing, however, you could end up with a mess like this – a car so awful it does not deserve to be displayed as a show car, never mind reach limited production. Intended to be available in limited numbers, Italian coachbuilder Castagna's Mini-based Crossup concept was more of a mess-up, proving to be rather more exclusive than the company had hoped for. Indeed, it is doubtful that any of these nasty conversions were ever actually carried out.

SPECIFICATION	
ORIGIN	Italy
DEBUT	Geneva 2005
ENGINE CAPACITY	1598cc (98cu in) supercharged
CONFIGURATION	Front-mounted four-cylinder
TRANSMISSION	Six-speed manual
POWER	127kW (170bhp)
TOP SPEED	209km/h (130mph)
LENGTH	4420mm (174in)
WIDTH	1730mm (68in)

Left: *The Crossup was created to demonstrate the coachbuilder Castagna's ability to create bespoke Mini-based vehicles for its customers.*

Any Mini could be used as the basis for a Castagna conversion; it was assumed a Cooper S would be chosen for its extra performance.

Alongside the Crossup was a Mini-based beach buggy called the Tender; Castagna could also build woody Mini estates too. Nice …

The reason why the Crossup was so ugly was that rear overhang – Castagna simply grafted an extra section onto the rear.

The pick-up bed was useless; other nasty styling affectations included the rear-mounted spare wheel and a grab handle around the rear window.

CITROËN CRUISE CROSSER *(2007)*

Think of all the six-wheeled production cars ever made and you have a pretty short list. Like a list of none. Now think of the six-wheeled show cars that never went anywhere and it is a list of every one ever made. From the Panther Six to the Wolfrace Sonic, all went down in history as lemons – and Citroën, with the help of Swiss oddball Franco Sbarro, decided to add to the tally with the Cruise Crosser. Not to be confused with Citroën's own in-house lemon the C-Crosser concept, the Cruise Crosser was a six-wheeled leviathan on a road to nowhere.

SPECIFICATION

ORIGIN	Switzerland/France
DEBUT	Geneva 2007
ENGINE CAPACITY	2.2 litres (134cu in) turbo
CONFIGURATION	Front-mounted diesel in-line four
TRANSMISSION	Six-speed manual, four- or six-wheel drive
POWER	139kW (186bhp) plus 20kW (27bhp) electric motor
TOP SPEED	N/A
LENGTH	N/A
WIDTH	N/A

Left: ***When the Cruise Crosser was unveiled in 2007, its maker claimed that it would be going into production within months. We're still waiting ...***

The concept was inspired by a series of automotive expeditions across Africa and Asia, including the first motor crossing of the Sahara in 1922.

A hybrid drivetrain combined a conventional diesel engine with an electric motor located under the rear floor.

With only the electric third axle being used for drive, it was possible to travel silently in 'Zero Emission Vehicle' mode.

Although there was seating for five inside, extra seats could be fitted onto that rear deck, or trans-Saharan kit could be carried.

CITROËN BERLINGO COUPÉ DE PLAGE (1996)

When Citroën introduced its Berlingo people-carrier in 1997, it let its designers loose to see what they could come up with – and boy did they go wild! Not. They started with the Berlingo Bulle, which offered little more than a reprofiled roof line, and followed up with the Berlingo Grand large – a standard car with two-tone trim and a sunroof. Cutting-edge stuff. So when you consider that the Coupé de Plage was by far and away the most creative of the three concepts, you get some idea of just how lame this trio was – which was particularly disappointing considering the company's brilliant past.

SPECIFICATION

ORIGIN	France
DEBUT	Paris 1996
ENGINE CAPACITY	1762cc (108cu in)
CONFIGURATION	Front-mounted four-cylinder
TRANSMISSION	Front-wheel drive
POWER	77kW (103bhp)
TOP SPEED	160km/h (100mph)
LENGTH	4110mm (162in)
WIDTH	1720mm (68in)

Left: *There was a load bay which could be used for carrying luggage, or a pair of deck chairs could be clipped in for some serious high-speed sunbathing.*

Looking like a pram handle, a support could be attached to the rear of the load bay for surfboards to be carried.

The mechanicals were standard Berlingo, which meant that there was a 1.8-litre (108cu in) engine driving the front wheels.

The cabin could accommodate only two passengers, while equipment levels were pretty basic by concept-car standards.

Citroën created bespoke three-spoke alloy wheels for the Berlingo de Plage; they looked like fan blades to add some dynamism.

CITROËN OSMOSE *(2000)*

It seems impossible to understand how any car maker could justify a car as ugly as the Osmose; the thought that anyone would be short-sighted enough to buy one is simply inconceivable. Citroën, however, reckoned that this was a 'bold concept which paints a vision of user-friendly vehicle design leading to a new form of relationship between pedestrians and motorists, while addressing the broader issue of responsible car use'. What that boiled down to was an almost unfeasibly unattractive car that was designed for car sharing on the fly. So not only did the Osmose fail aesthetically, but it was also doomed to fail because people have an aversion to picking up strangers thumbing a lift.

SPECIFICATION

ORIGIN	France
DEBUT	Paris 2000
ENGINE CAPACITY	N/A
CONFIGURATION	Petrol (gasoline)/ electric hybrid
TRANSMISSION	N/A
POWER	N/A
TOP SPEED	N/A
LENGTH	N/A
WIDTH	N/A

Left: *It was possible to book an Osmose using mobile (cell) phone technology; pedestrians sent out an alert, and nearby Osmose drivers would pick it up.*

The Osmose's driver could advertise on the side of the car the fact that he or she was happy to pick up hitchhikers.

There was room for three up front with their luggage behind, or the rear portion could be converted into two extra seats.

The outside of the car featured a series of airbags, to help reduce injuries to pedestrians should they be struck by an Osmose.

Most of the car's upper half was made of glass; it looked hideous but visibility was great. There was a huge sliding door on each side.

DODGE MAXXCAB *(2000)*

Pick-up trucks are designed for carrying stuff, while passenger cars – saloons (sedans) and hatchbacks, SUVs and MPVs – are designed for carrying people. So when Dodge unveiled the 'world's first passenger-priority pick-up truck you just knew that here was a vehicle which offered the worst of all worlds. Offering rather less usefulness than a decent estate car (station wagon), and nothing like the practicality of a conventional pick-up, the Maxxcab was fundamentally flawed from the outset. Still, as Dodge is a branch of the Chrysler Group, you should not be overly surprised about this – and we should all be grateful that it was never signed off for production.

SPECIFICATION

ORIGIN	USA
DEBUT	Detroit 2000
ENGINE CAPACITY	4700cc (287cu in)
CONFIGURATION	Front-mounted V8
TRANSMISSION	Four-speed auto, four-wheel drive
POWER	179kW (240bhp)
TOP SPEED	183km/h (114mph)
LENGTH	5156mm (209in)
WIDTH	2032mm (80in)

Left: *Inside the Maxxcab, the centre console housed a pop-up laptop computer, hooked up to LCDs in the instrument panel and the rear of the console.*

A 42-volt electrical system was installed, to better cope with all of the powered gadgetry fitted throughout.

There were three individual rear seats, with the middle one able to be moved backwards and forwards electrically.

As you would expect of such a huge vehicle, there were some substantial wheels attached; they measured 457mm (18in) across.

Dodge claimed that the Maxxcab could be used as an 'office on wheels' or a 'mobile daycare centre'. So why the pick-up configuration?

EDAG LUV (2007)

Automotive oxymorons are nothing new, but this must rate as one of the most bizarre ever. EDAG had already unveiled a string of bizarre creations before it came up with this – the Luxury Utility Vehicle. If you had to come up with two words at opposite ends of a spectrum, 'luxury' and 'utility' would be pretty safe choices. One conjures up images of unbridled comfort, without too much of a focus on practicality, while the other offers connotations of carrying bales of hay and having a mud-soaked interior. So trying to marry the two was always going to be a hopeless exercise – not that this stopped EDAG from making the attempt.

SPECIFICATION

ORIGIN	Germany
DEBUT	Geneva 2007
ENGINE CAPACITY	6.1 litres (372cu in)
CONFIGURATION	Front-mounted V8
TRANSMISSION	Four-wheel drive
POWER	345kW (462bhp)
TOP SPEED	In excess of 250km/h (155mph)
LENGTH	N/A
WIDTH	N/A

Left: *The LUV was intended to mix carry-all practicality with unbridled luxury for five. It was effectively a twin-cab pick-up.*

There was a nautical flavour to the LUV, as the pick-up load bay, bonnet (hood) and interior all featured polished teak.

Brabus was one of EDAG's partners in crime for the project; the tuning company supplied an upgraded 6.1-litre (372cu in) Mercedes V8.

The 559 x 254mm (22 x 10in) alloy wheels also came from Brabus; they were wrapped in super-sticky 295/35 ZR22 Yokohama tyres.

The brakes were impressive; there were 12-piston callipers up front with 380mm (15in) discs; at the rear were six-pot callipers with 355mm (14in) discs.

FIAT OLTRE (2005)

SUVs were at the height of their popularity in the early twenty-first century, so you cannot blame Fiat for trying to get in on the act with one of the most ridiculously oversized 4x4s ever. Doing a Hummer, however, was just what Fiat did not need; here was a company best known for its small cars, and the smaller the better. If it was built for the city and packed a 1.2-litre (73cu in) engine, Fiat was on safe ground, so something the size of an aircraft carrier was not recommended. It seems that Fiat got the message because it did not develop the Oltre at all, helped by the fact that the Italian outfit was on the verge of bankruptcy when the 4x4 was unveiled.

SPECIFICATION

ORIGIN	Italy
DEBUT	Bologna 2005
ENGINE CAPACITY	3000cc (183cu in) turbocharged
CONFIGURATION	Front-mounted diesel four-cylinder
TRANSMISSION	Six-speed manual, four-wheel drive
POWER	140kW (185bhp)
TOP SPEED	130km/h (81mph)
LENGTH	4870mm (192in)
WIDTH	2200mm (87in)

Left: *Fiat was convinced that the Oltre had 'exuberant styling'. That would be one way of putting it; others would say that it was ugly, over the top, hideous ...*

Some parts of the Oltre appeared unfinished; it looked as if the vehicle's bodyshell was designed for a completely different chassis.

The Oltre was based on Iveco's LMV (Light Multi-Role Vehicle), which was developed for military off-road use.

Unbelievably, the door handles were recessed so 'they did not constitute an obstacle when driving off-road'. This on a car 2200mm (87in) wide!

While there was a double cab capable of seating up to five people, the back was left exposed in pick-up fashion.

FORD 24.7 *(2000)*

There was so much garbage talked about the 24.7 upon its unveiling that it is hard to know where to start. Choice quotes include: '24.7 is not just transportation, it's about guiding you through life'; '24.7 promises to do for personal transportation what the computer has done for the office'; and the laughable 'the 24.7 pick-up is ready for any user adventure – whether it is climbing rocks by day or listening to a favorite band at night'. In truth, this was a car that was completely pointless – it did not do anything that a normal production car could not do, so Ford just talked in sweeping terms about how it was going to revolutionize personal transport. It didn't, of course.

SPECIFICATION

ORIGIN	USA
DEBUT	Detroit 2000
ENGINE CAPACITY	2 litres (122cu in)
CONFIGURATION	Front-mounted four-cylinder
TRANSMISSION	Front-wheel drive
POWER	82kW (110bhp)
TOP SPEED	N/A
LENGTH	N/A
WIDTH	N/A

Left: *There were three 24.7s made: a pick-up, a 'wagon' (which was really a compact SUV) and a coupé (which in turn was effectively a three-door compact SUV).*

One of the key aspects of the 24.7 was how it could be personalized, especially the dash display, which could be configured in numerous ways.

Many of the car's features – such as the telephone or entertainment system – could be set up or controlled using voice activation.

All three of the 24.7s featured 432mm (17in) six-spoke matte aluminum finished wheels wrapped in specially cut 245/50R-17 Goodyear tyres.

The lighting system was claimed to be so reliable that it would last the lifetime of the car; much of it used light-emitting diodes.

GMC DENALI XT *(2008)*

Talk about fiddling while Rome burned – it is no wonder that General Motors went belly up soon after its GMC Denali XT was unveiled. As consumers moved into smaller cars thanks to spiralling fuel prices, here was GM unveiling a massive car that was neither fish nor fowl. It was not a luxury car, nor was it an SUV or even a pick-up, yet it had elements of all three – with a bit of lead-sled thrown in for good measure, with what looked like a roof chop. To be fair, GM was not the only one guilty of continuing to ignore environmental concerns, producing one leviathan after another – but at least most efforts from rivals were vaguely useful, unlike this.

SPECIFICATION

ORIGIN	USA
DEBUT	Chicago 2008
ENGINE CAPACITY	4.9 litres (299cu in)
CONFIGURATION	Front-mounted petrol (gasoline)/ E85 V8
TRANSMISSION	Two-mode hybrid
POWER	243kW (326bhp)
TOP SPEED	N/A
LENGTH	5207mm (205in)
WIDTH	1938mm (76in)

Left: ***Despite the Denali XT's massive dimensions, its payload was a laughable 499kg (1100lb). It could also tow just 1587kg (3500lb), about the same as a mid-sized family car is capable of.***

GM claimed that the XT was environmentally friendly because it could burn E85 fuel and featured a hybrid power pack – but it was no lightweight.

The pick-up bed measured just 1397 x 1206mm (55 x 47½in), ensuring that it was not really large enough to carry anything worthwhile.

The cabin was luxurious, with leather trim for all visible surfaces, with lashings of alloy highlights to brighten things up.

Even though the XT was pointless, it looked good with its low roof line, LED headlights and 584mm (23in) wheels at each corner.

IAD HUNTER (1988)

Practicality does not always have to feature too highly on the agenda of the concept-car designer, but any car, concept or otherwise, should still be of some use to somebody, somewhere. It seems that this salient fact was not communicated to the guys at IAD, who unleashed this utterly irrelevant machine on the world in 1988. This sport-leisure utility vehicle did not look too bad, but it does not take much further inspection to see that it offers no weather protection and little in the way of roll protection, and it forces its occupants to wear restrictive helmets on the move. While there may have been some who thought that this constituted fun, they were already tucked up in a padded cell.

SPECIFICATION

ORIGIN	UK
DEBUT	Turin 1988
ENGINE CAPACITY	2792cc (170cu in)
CONFIGURATION	Front-mounted V6
TRANSMISSION	Five-speed manual, four-wheel drive
POWER	112kW (150bhp)
TOP SPEED	N/A
LENGTH	4143mm (163in)
WIDTH	1908mm (75in)

Left: ***IAD teamed up with Philips to integrate a six-speaker hi-fi system into the Hunter. There was also a DAT (Digital Audio Tape) system. Oh dear ...***

Under the skin were Ford Sierra XR4x4 mechanicals, which meant a 2.8-litre (170cu in) V6 engine and four-wheel drive.

A CARIN satellite navigation system was fitted. At the time, this could not be made to work – but functionality would not be far away …

There were just two moulded seats, each moulded in Sorboskin – whatever that was. The door trims were identically covered.

The tailgate was split, with the lower half forming a drop-down step and the upper portion side-hinged for access to the load bay.

ITALDESIGN/FIAT FORMULA 4 *(1996)*

Italdesign set out with good intentions when it created the Formula 4 – it wanted to create an affordable sportscar for young drivers, which is a very laudable aim. So what a shame this was the result; a horrible conglomeration of old and new that was madly impractical and grotesquely contrived. Italdesign claimed that the Formula 4 conjured up images of Formula One, but with space for four – hence the name. The only thing that this concept had in common with a typical Formula One machine, however, was that it was madly impractical thanks to a complete lack of weather protection. Other than that, it was hard to see any connection.

SPECIFICATION

ORIGIN	Italy
DEBUT	Turin 1996
ENGINE CAPACITY	1998cc (122cu in)
CONFIGURATION	Front-mounted five-cylinder
TRANSMISSION	Five-speed manual, front-wheel drive
POWER	110kW (147bhp)
TOP SPEED	N/A
LENGTH	4155mm (164in)
WIDTH	1820mm (72in)

Left: *Whatever else it was, the Formula 4 was eminently customizable, including a choice of grilles, wheels, headlights, aeroscreens and interior finishes.*

The car was split into four sections – one for each occupant. They each got a roll bar, four-point harness and airbag.

No weather protection at all was provided, which is why all of the materials used to trim the interior were waterproof.

A single exhaust pipe exited from the rear of the car, and for some odd reason Italdesign chose to fit external boot (trunk) lid hinges.

Some of the nastier details include the very retro wire wheels, tacky stick-on rear spoiler and those hideous pre-war aeroscreens.

ITALDESIGN MACHIMOTO (1986)

When you are as prolific as Giorgetto Giugiaro, you would have to be superhuman to get it right every time. But there is making a mistake and there is coming up with a total disaster such as the Machimoto. A cross between a car and a motorbike, the Machimoto was intended to provide cheap transport for up to nine people in developing countries – clearly comfort was not expected to be too high on the agenda. As if all this were not bad enough, the same design house would later make a similar mistake with the introduction of the Formula 4 (see pages 162–3).

SPECIFICATION

ORIGIN	Italy
DEBUT	Turin 1986
ENGINE CAPACITY	1781cc (109cu in)
CONFIGURATION	Front-mounted four-cylinder
TRANSMISSION	Five-speed manual, front-wheel drive
POWER	104kW (139bhp)
TOP SPEED	N/A
LENGTH	3985mm (157in)
WIDTH	1680mm (66in)

Left: ***Each occupant had a handlebar to hold on to and a lap belt to hold them in position; it cannot possibly have been comfortable!***

In basic form there were two rows of three seats, which were more like saddles. A smaller row for three children was also squeezed in.

The basic construction of the Machimoto was via a series of steel tubes, which were then wrapped in silver-coloured plastic panels.

As if carrying nine people does not sound unsafe enough in a car this size, that roll bar could be removed altogether for maximum danger.

The oily bits were taken straight from the VW Golf GTi 16-valve, which meant a 1.8-litre (109cu in) engine driving the front wheels.

ITALDESIGN HELMUT NEWTON (2001)

It is said that there is no accounting for taste, and if you want the proof then here it is. When iconic photographer Helmut Newton saw Italdesign's Touareg concept at the 2000 Turin motor show, he fell in love with it – so much that he asked the design house if it would build a street-legal example just for him. The original concept looked just like the one you see here: ugly in the extreme and as subtle as a punch in the face. Italdesign could not resist the temptation to fulfil Newton's request, giving him his road-ready car in time for his eightieth birthday.

SPECIFICATION

ORIGIN	Italy
DEBUT	2001
ENGINE CAPACITY	2972cc (183cu in)
CONFIGURATION	Front-mounted V6
TRANSMISSION	Four-wheel drive
POWER	112kW (150bhp)
TOP SPEED	N/A
LENGTH	4140mm (163in)
WIDTH	1850mm (73in)

Left: *The Newton took its mechanicals from Mitsubishi's Shogu 4x4, with the result that it featured a four-wheel drive system just as the Touareg had done.*

The original concept featured V8 petrol (gasoline) power, but the road car was fitted with a Mitsubishi-sourced V6 engine instead.

All those tubes are not just for show; between them they make up the Newton's structure because there is no monocoque as such.

There was room for four in comfort (that's relative comfort, of course) or five at a pinch – two in the front and up to three in the back.

Everything was made of steel, from the various tubes to the panels – the latter being constructed from stainless steel.

JEEP TREO *(2003)*

Has there ever been a more confused concept-car proposal than this one? Here was Jeep, a brand renowned for its go-anywhere 4x4s, creating a three-seater supermini suited only for road use, thanks to minimal ground clearance. Yet there were still massive wheels and four-wheel drive, plus one of the least space-efficient designs ever conceived. Despite the footprint of a normal car, the Treo's cabin was short and narrow, thanks to a mass of wasted space all around it. It is hard to see just who the Treo was aimed at, as a raft of compromises made it unsuitable for just about anybody.

SPECIFICATION

ORIGIN	USA
DEBUT	Tokyo 2003
ENGINE CAPACITY	N/A
CONFIGURATION	Hydrogen fuel cell
TRANSMISSION	Four-wheel drive
POWER	N/A
TOP SPEED	N/A
LENGTH	3235mm (127in)
WIDTH	1680mm (66in)

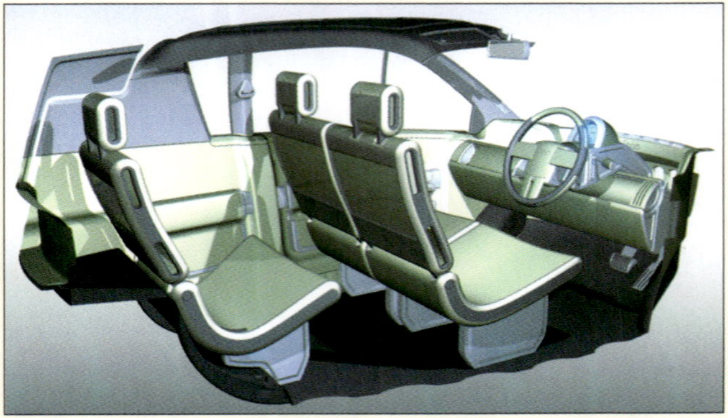

Left: ***The lightweight seats were made of a translucent material over a carbon-fibre frame. The rear seat folded flat for extra storage space if needed.***

There was drive-by-wire, with a hydrogen fuel cell driving all four wheels via an electric-drive powertrain.

There was an unusual 3+1 seating layout, with two seats up front and an occasional seat in the middle behind them.

The only clue to the Treo's origins was the classic seven-bar grille that had featured on all of the company's cars.

To deal with speed bumps and poor road surfaces, there were 483mm (19in) alloy wheels front and rear, with 185/65 tyres.

KARMANN SUC (2005)

Karmann bit the dust in 2009, and it is not hard to see why, when it was focusing its efforts on projects as worthless as this one. If ever there were a type of car guaranteed to prove impossible to resolve economically, it is the four-door convertible. Throw in the SUV configuration as a starting point, and you just know that you are doomed to fail. Still, that did not stop Karmann dreaming up the Sport Utility Cabrio, in conjunction with transmission specialist ZF. The duo had its work cut out trying to overcome the packaging, rigidity and safety issues inherent in a car such as this.

SPECIFICATION

ORIGIN	Germany
DEBUT	Frankfurt 2005
ENGINE CAPACITY	4401cc (269cu in)
CONFIGURATION	Front-mounted V8
TRANSMISSION	Six-speed auto, four-wheel drive
POWER	239kW (320bhp)
TOP SPEED	N/A
LENGTH	4638mm (183in)
WIDTH	2180mm (86in)

Left: *As if making a convertible four-door was not enough of a challenge, there was no B-pillar; the rear doors of Karmann's SUC opened backwards.*

Behind the rear seats there was a pair of pop-up roll hoops, for protection in the event of the car rolling.

The folding cloth roof was a masterpiece, as it incorporated a polycarbonate sunroof – yet it still folded flush when stowed.

All of the running gear was taken from the BMW X5, which meant that there was a V8 petrol (gasoline) engine and four-wheel drive.

Also ingenious was the glass rear window, which retracted electrically into the tailgate when the roof was stowed.

MATRA M72 *(2002)*

This car was so bad, it could almost have been part of the MG-Rover line-up. No, really. MG-Rover had discussions with Matra, with a view to selling the M72 in some countries. Instead, MG-Rover focused on the gem that was the CityRover, a rebadged Tata that was universally slated. But things could have been so different; the company could have been in on this four-wheeled catastrophe instead, developed by Matra and 'totally in phase with today's consumer', according to Matra. With judgment like that, it is no wonder that, within a few short years of the M72's unveiling, both Matra and MG-Rover would be footnotes in the history books.

SPECIFICATION

ORIGIN	France
DEBUT	Geneva 2002
ENGINE CAPACITY	749cc (46cu in)
CONFIGURATION	Front-mounted two-cylinder
TRANSMISSION	Continuously variable transmission
POWER	37kW (50bhp)
TOP SPEED	130km/h (81mph)
LENGTH	3237mm (127in)
WIDTH	1564mm (62in)

Left: *Strictly speaking, this was not a concept. Rather, it was a prototype that Matra hoped to put into production. Predictably, nobody wanted it.*

The interior was minimalist, with two bucket seats and only very basic instrumentation. It had to be simple, as there was no weather protection.

Matra claimed that the M72 was a cross between a car and a motorbike, offering the best of both worlds. In reality, it offered the worst of both.

The M72's design was an overly fussy mess, with details crammed in wherever they would fit – and often also where they did not.

Two versions of the M72 were proposed: a 15kW (20bhp) edition for teen drivers and a 37kW (50bhp) one for older drivers who had no shame.

MAZDA SECRET HIDEOUT (2001)

It is amazing what a fertile imagination can conjure up. Anybody else would call this a van – or, if they were pushing their luck, a cross between a van and an estate car (station wagon) with very thick rear pillars. Not Mazda, though, which claimed its Secret Hideout concept offered 'stylish and insightful design' while being 'innovative and functional'. As was common with Japanese car makers at the time, the truth was that this was a car which was designed to offer a social space for its occupants, thanks to a flexible cabin and terrible outward visibility – ensuring even worse inward visibility.

SPECIFICATION

ORIGIN	Japan
DEBUT	Tokyo 2001
ENGINE CAPACITY	1.3 litres (79cu in)
CONFIGURATION	Front-mounted four-cylinder
TRANSMISSION	Front-wheel drive
POWER	N/A
TOP SPEED	N/A
LENGTH	N/A
WIDTH	N/A

Left: *The key to the Mazda Secret Hideout was its very thick rear pillar, allowing a degree of privacy for the Japanese youth at which it was aimed.*

A cutting-edge entertainment system offered Bluetooth and a 'portable media support system' – whatever that was.

There were several retro touches, such as an alloy windscreen surround and exposed mudguards for the wheels.

The cabin featured front and rear seats that could be folded completely flat, to create a single level surface throughout.

There was just one door on the driver's side, but two on the passengers', the rear one being a 'Freestyle' reverse-hinged affair.

MINI TRAVELLER (2005)

We received our first glimpse of BMW's Mini Clubman when it was revealed as the Mini Concept at the 2005 Frankfurt motor show. It looked pretty good, too, with its pillarless design and reasonably uncluttered lines. Just two months later at the Tokyo motor show, however, this monstrosity was unveiled to the world – and what a mess it was. Unbelievably overdesigned, this new concept was simply called Concept Tokyo because BMW did not know who owned the rights to the 'Traveller' and 'Countryman' names. By the time the car saw production, it was named Clubman and featured rather simpler lines – although it was still overdesigned.

SPECIFICATION

ORIGIN	Germany
DEBUT	Tokyo 2005
ENGINE CAPACITY	1.6 litres (98cu in)
CONFIGURATION	Front-mounted four-cylinder
TRANSMISSION	Five-speed manual, front-wheel drive
POWER	N/A
TOP SPEED	N/A
LENGTH	3815mm (150in)
WIDTH	2540mm (100in)

Left: *The Traveller was a homage to all things British, as it was set up to cater for people who wanted to drink tea while watching a game of cricket or a chukka or two of polo.*

Perhaps the most kitsch design element was the flip-down panel in the side of the car, which exposed the tea bags and hot-water flask.

There was a strange wooden disc set into the Traveller's roof; it was a pull-out table, which also came with a pair of folding chairs.

If there is one thing that marks out an over-the-top car, it is lots of gold detailing – such as on the Traveller's wheels, grille and front wings (fenders).

Compared with the regular Mini hatch, the Traveller's wheelbase was stretched by 80mm (3.14in), while there was an extra 100mm (4in) of rear overhang.

NISSAN TERRANAUT (2006)

By definition, building a lunar rover for anywhere on Earth is pointless. Yet that is what Nissan set out to achieve with its Terranaut mobile science laboratory. Designed to protect its occupants from the extremes of the world's environments, according to Nissan, the Terranaut 'has been designed for observation and communication in all four corners of the world'. To be fair, the Terranaut did look very cool with its chunky lines, high-tech looks and generous dimensions. But despite all this, the Terranaut was still an utterly absurd proposition and a distraction from Nissan attempting to solve automotive problems that affected the real world.

SPECIFICATION

ORIGIN	Japan
DEBUT	Geneva 2006
ENGINE CAPACITY	N/A
CONFIGURATION	Front-mounted
TRANSMISSION	Four-wheel drive
POWER	N/A
TOP SPEED	N/A
LENGTH	4965mm (195in)
WIDTH	2100mm (83in)

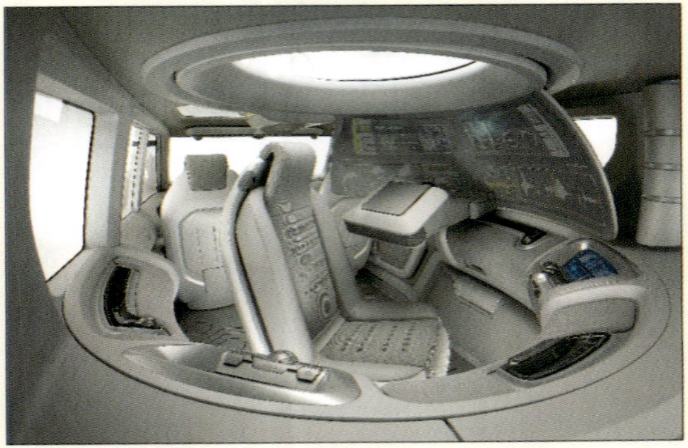

Left: *Despite the Terranaut's generous external dimensions, there was room for just three inside; the cabin was stuffed with high-tech gadgets instead.*

Just three doors were fitted; there were two on the passenger side, but just the one on the driver's side.

Behind the two front seats was a single swivelling seat, which sat under a glass roof-mounted dome for external observation.

The paint used aircraft technology and was able to withstand extremes of temperature. The off-white finish contrasted with the bronze glass.

Those wheels were 483mm (19in) in diameter; they were wrapped in puncture-proof tyres that could be used on- or off-road.

PEUGEOT 806 RUNABOUT (1997)

People-carriers often handle like a boat, but Peugeot got carried away with this theory when it created its 806 Runabout. A cross between Peugeot's 806 people-carrier and a speedboat, the Runabout was contrived and ridiculous – and those were among its better points. In the transformation to Runabout, the 806 lost its people-carrying abilities, as well as any semblance of practicality. The latter omission is no bad thing in a concept, but Peugeot clearly had ideas above its station in the Runabout's brochure; the company talked of the rich driving to their yachts on the French Riviera and in the harbours of Florida. Really? In a Peugeot?

SPECIFICATION

ORIGIN	France
DEBUT	Frankfurt 1997
ENGINE CAPACITY	2946cc (180cu in)
CONFIGURATION	Front-mounted V6
TRANSMISSION	Four-speed auto, front-wheel drive
POWER	145kW (194bhp)
TOP SPEED	N/A
LENGTH	4750mm (187in)
WIDTH	1960mm (77in)

Left: *The glasshouse treatment on Peugeot's Runabout was one of the strongest nautical links, as it appeared to have been lifted straight from a speedboat.*

The Runabout was definitely suitable for sunny climes only – there was no form of weather protection whatsoever.

Another of the Runabout's nautical touches was the load bay behind the two seats, which was finished in slatted solid varnished teak.

Power was provided by Peugeot's new 3-litre (180cu in) V6 engine, driving the front wheels via a four-speed automatic gearbox.

The concept stuck with Peugeot's standard production alloy wheels, but here they were wrapped in specially designed and constructed tyres.

PEUGEOT 607 PALADINE (2000)

As soon as Peugeot unveiled its large 607 saloon (sedan) to the world, it was instantly forgotten. When it comes to guaranteed sales flops, big French saloons are up there with anything packing six wheels, amphibious capabilities or purely electric propulsion. In other words – a nonstarter. Yet that did not prevent Peugeot from introducing the 607, guaranteeing that something further would have to follow, to remind people of the car's existence. That something was this – a landaulette edition with a fixed roof over the front seats and a folding roof over the rears. It was a reasonably neat solution, but dictators did not queue to trade in their Mercs and Maybachs.

SPECIFICATION

ORIGIN	France
DEBUT	Geneva 2000
ENGINE CAPACITY	2946cc (180cu in)
CONFIGURATION	Front-mounted V6
TRANSMISSION	Four-speed auto, front-wheel drive
POWER	145kW (194bhp)
TOP SPEED	N/A
LENGTH	4902mm (193in)
WIDTH	1835mm (72in)

Left: *Landaulettes traditionally feature a fixed roof over the front seats and a folding cloth roof over the rear; the Paladine featured a folding hardtop instead.*

Both of the rear seats could be reclined electrically. There were also adjustable footrests and headrests, all electrically adjusted.

Inside, there was seating for five, with two chairs in the front, two in the back and a rear-facing occasional seat, also in the back.

In the nose was Peugeot's 3-litre (180cu in) V6 engine. Unusually for a car of this size, it drove the front wheels.

The alloy wheels had a diameter of 457mm (18in). They were covered in specially made 235/45 puncture-proof tyres.

PININFARINA X (1960)

In modern parlance, they really thought outside the box with this one. Iconic, revolutionary – offer up all the clichés you want – this concept was utterly irrelevant, as just about none of the styling themes or technologies it introduced stayed the course. In terms of the mechanical layout, packaging and styling trends, this car offered a foretaste of a future that simply did not happen because it was just too fanciful. One area in which the Pininfarina X did succeed was in creating a low-drag shape – this was one hell of an aerodynamic car. So it is just a shame that it looked like a cut-and-shut that had been welded together using five different vehicles.

SPECIFICATION

ORIGIN	Italy
DEBUT	Turin 1960
ENGINE CAPACITY	1089cc (66cu in)
CONFIGURATION	Rear-mounted four-cylinder
TRANSMISSION	Four-speed manual, rear-wheel drive
POWER	32kW (43bhp)
TOP SPEED	146km/h (91mph)
LENGTH	4300mm (169in)
WIDTH	1715mm (68in)

Left: ***There was only one wheel at the rear, as the wheels were laid out in a diamond formation and, as there was no rear-wheel drive, a differential was not needed.***

Everything was flush, from the headlights and windscreen, to the fuel filler flap and tiny overriders fitted in place of bumpers.

Power was provided by a 1.1-litre (66cu in) Fiat four-cylinder engine, which was frugal and pokey enough to give a 146km/h (91mph) top speed.

Those pronounced fins at the rear were there to aid high-speed stability – they were not added as a styling exercise.

The front wheel was used for steering, while those towards the middle (but very much towards the back) simply offered stability.

RINSPEED PRESTO *(2002)*

It would be easy to include in this book just about any concept Rinspeed has ever produced. The Swiss outfit has always been divorced from reality, offering one madcap concept after another and always packing some completely unnecessary technology or design feature. For the Presto the pièce de resistance was an ability to be shortened or lengthened at will. Like the Renault Zoom elsewhere in these pages, the Presto was meant to offer the best of all worlds: a compact car for the city and a more spacious one for longer runs. The unavoidable reality, of course, was that such technology was a complete nonstarter because of its cost and complexity.

SPECIFICATION

ORIGIN	Switzerland
DEBUT	Geneva 2002
ENGINE CAPACITY	1689cc (103cu in) turbocharged
CONFIGURATION	Front-mounted diesel four-cylinder
TRANSMISSION	Front-wheel drive
POWER	89kW (120bhp)
TOP SPEED	182km/h (113mph)
LENGTH	2996–3742mm (118–147in)
WIDTH	1847mm (73in)

Left: *In short-wheelbase form the Presto had seating for just two; at the press of a button it could be transformed into a two-seater.*

The engine was taken from the Mercedes A-Class; it was a 1.7-litre (103cu in) turbodiesel unit in the nose, driving the front wheels.

This engine was a dual-fuel unit, designed to be run on a mixture of diesel and natural gas for very low sulphur emissions.

The tail lighting was by LED. Upon braking, the word 'Stop' was spelt out; when indicating, the word 'Turn' appeared on the rear panel.

The Presto's seats were taken from Smart's parts bin, while the dashboard was borrowed from the Mercedes A-Class, all finished in orange.

RINSPEED SENSO *(2005)*

How's this for pointless – a car that monitors its driver's biometric data and adjusts various parameters to suit? As a result, its creator called this the 'most sensuous car in the world' – something that Toyota may have taken issue with, thanks to the development of its Pod, seen elsewhere in this book. The Senso took into account the driver's pulse and driving behaviour, then adjusted the music, interior lighting and even the fragrances to suit. As a result, it could soothe a frustrated driver or pep up a tired one; Rinspeed did not say what it could do for a driver both frustrated and tired …

SPECIFICATION

ORIGIN	Switzerland
DEBUT	Geneva 2005
ENGINE CAPACITY	3179cc (194cu in)
CONFIGURATION	Mid-mounted flat-six
TRANSMISSION	Six-speed manual, rear-wheel drive
POWER	186kW (250bhp)
TOP SPEED	250km/h (155mph)
LENGTH	4475mm (176in)
WIDTH	1820mm (72in)

Left: *With a kerb weight of 1385kg (3053lb) and 300Nm (221lbf ft) of torque up for grabs, the Senso could manage 0–100km/h (0–62mph) in just 5.9 seconds.*

Despite its 3.2-litre (194cu in) Porsche Boxster engine, the Senso was green; it ran on natural gas and its bodywork was fully recyclable.

Four small LCD monitors could emit stimulating (orange/yellow), relaxing (blue/violet) or neutral (green) colour patterns into the driver's line of vision.

Fragrances could be pumped into the car through the air vents. Vanilla-mandarin was used for its calming effect, citrus-grapefruit for stimulation.

There were 483mm (19in) Barracuda alloy wheels all round, shod with Continental SportContact 35-profile tyres.

RINSPEED X DREAM (1999)

Even by Rinspeed's standards this was a truly irrelevant concept, as it was an outrageously powerful pick-up that offered little in the way of comfort or protection from the elements, while also coming with its own hovercraft. A pretty mainstream market, in that case. To be fair, the hovercraft was intended to be merely representative of the type of thing the X Dream could carry; it could easily be substituted for a jet-ski, hot-air balloon or similar leisure toy. While the concept of the X Dream may have appealed to a few people, it is extremely unlikely that those hideous lines or the complete lack of practicality would have had the same effect.

SPECIFICATION

ORIGIN	Switzerland
DEBUT	Geneva 1999
ENGINE CAPACITY	5439cc (332cu in)
CONFIGURATION	Front-mounted V8
TRANSMISSION	Five-speed auto, four-wheel drive
POWER	259kW (347bhp)
TOP SPEED	237km/h (147mph)
LENGTH	5780mm (228in)
WIDTH	2195mm (86in)

Left: *To enable easy loading and unloading of the pick-up bed, an electro-hydraulic swivelling crane was fitted along the back edge. Just what every vehicle needs.*

Despite a bodyshell made of carbon-fibre for maximum strength with minimum weight, the X Dream still tipped the scales at 1860kg (4100lb).

In true Rinspeed form there was maximum complexity; in place of a fixed windscreen there were individual aeroscreens, each electrically adjustable.

With a Mercedes-sourced 5.5-litre (332cu in) V8, the top speed was a claimed 237km/h (147mph) – which would have been truly frightening.

Styling was not an X Dream strong point; the grille was ridiculously oversized, while overall it looked as if the car had been left in the sun, where it had melted.

TOYOTA AYGO DJ (2005)

When it comes to pointless cars, few can top the Toyota Aygo DJ. Designed for the disc jockey on the move, the DJ was built to promote the launch of Toyota's new city car, at the 2005 Geneva motor show. As Toyota put it, this was less of a car and more of a music machine because the Aygo was completely re-engineered to become a mobile pro-DJ mixing desk. Unfortunately, so many compromises were made in the transition that while the DJ was great for those who needed to make music, it was not so great for those who needed to get from A to B. Which kind of defeats the purpose of a car, really.

SPECIFICATION

ORIGIN	Japan
DEBUT	Geneva 2005
ENGINE CAPACITY	998cc (61cu in)
CONFIGURATION	Front-mounted three-cylinder
TRANSMISSION	Five-speed manual, front-wheel drive
POWER	51kW (68bhp)
TOP SPEED	N/A
LENGTH	3405mm (134in)
WIDTH	1675mm (66in)

Left: *As if the whole concept of the DJ was not impractical enough, the rear suspensions had to be removed to accommodate the mechanism for the slide-out back end.*

Four mid-sized and tweeter speakers were built into each of the rear doors, with two 30cm (12in) subwoofers in the vacant spare-wheel well.

To make the DJ stand out, there was a one-off bodykit plus orange-and-black paintwork; even the front and rear lights were black.

Despite all the extra weight, the DJ was fitted with a standard Aygo engine, ensuring decidedly leisurely performance.

The whole rear section of the car extended to reveal twin turntables and a mixing desk, plus a double CD mixer desk.

TOYOTA CELICA CRUISING DECK *(1999)*

If you were asked to come up with two types of car at opposite ends of the spectrum, it is a pretty safe bet that you would choose a combination something like a sportscar and a pick-up. After all, one is built purely for the fun of driving and the other exists to earn its keep, lugging stuff from one place to another. So if you were to try to combine these two car types into one, you would be guaranteed to fail to come up with anything remotely convincing. That did not stop Toyota giving it a go, though, with its lamentable Celica Cruising Deck, which was effectively a pick-up with a pop-up seat in the back. Very nasty indeed.

SPECIFICATION

ORIGIN	Japan
DEBUT	Tokyo 1999
ENGINE CAPACITY	1794cc (109cu in)
CONFIGURATION	Front-mounted four-cylinder
TRANSMISSION	Six-speed manual, front-wheel drive
POWER	139kW (187bhp)
TOP SPEED	225km/h (140mph)
LENGTH	4425mm (174in)
WIDTH	1735mm (68in)

Left: *The Cruising Deck was not officially a pick-up, but with its side-hinged tailgate and fold-flat rear seats, that's essentially what it amounted to – unfortunately.*

The mechanicals were taken from the then-new seventh-generation Celica, which meant a 1.8-litre (109cu in) twin-cam four-cylinder engine.

There was no weather protection at all for those seated in the back; this was definitely a car for sunny climes only.

That massive rear spoiler doubled as the platform onto which the headrests were positioned, for those on display in the back.

The Cruising Deck was inspired by the roadsters of the 1920s, with the dickie seats that turned the rear of the car into a convertible.

MADLY IMPRACTICAL

If the last batch of concepts were pointless, this lot takes such an idea to a whole new level. For example, a wheel at each corner has worked for decades, offering stability and control – so why then offer a diamond formation, as the Assystem did, which was worse in every way? Bodywork is another one. Fabric bodies were common in the 1920s, but they were costly to fabricate, fragile and offered relatively limited possibilities when it came to styling. But that did not stop BMW dispensing with plastic or metal in its quest for a fabric body.

Elsewhere in the chapter you will discover nonsensical power sources, ludicrously complex (and costly) construction techniques and a raft of cars that offered solution to problems that simply didn't exist. In a world where reduced production costs through simplified construction processes is the norm, somebody seems to have forgotten to tell this bunch of designers. As a result, the chances of any of these concepts – or even just their key design features – reaching production are impossibly remote.

Left: *The Eclectic was Venturi's idea of green transport; its impracticality meant you were better off walking.*

ASSYSTEM CITY CAR *(2008)*

Built in conjunction with crazy Swiss car builder Franco Sbarro, the Assystem was billed as an 'intelligent city car'. To be fair, it did incorporate some interesting technologies, and it did not stick slavishly to the rules just because everyone else was doing so. The Assystem also appeared, however, to do things differently just for the sake of it – that diamond wheel formation, for example, was utterly bizarre and guaranteed to lead to great difficulties when it came to designing an attractive bodyshell. Which must have been why they gave up on that score at the first hurdle. This car redefined ugly.

SPECIFICATION

ORIGIN	France
DEBUT	Geneva 2008
ENGINE CAPACITY	600cc (37cu in)
CONFIGURATION	Rear-mounted two-cylinder
TRANSMISSION	Automatic, rear-wheel drive
POWER	45kW (60bhp)
TOP SPEED	130km/h (81mph)
LENGTH	N/A
WIDTH	N/A

Left: ***The Assystem's windscreen could be turned into a giant TV screen, offering the driver an enhanced view ahead in darkness and poor weather.***

There was seating for just two – which is one more than most cars have on board when used for the daily commute.

For all-round visibility there were cameras covering the full 360 degrees around the car. Images were relayed onto the in-dash screen.

To prevent the Assystem being stolen, a camera analysed the driver's iris before allowing the engine to be started.

The front wheel turned, but the two in the middle and the one at the rear were fixed. This supposedly allowed greater agility.

BMW GINA (2008)

Trying to come up with the least practical construction for a car? If so, there is a good chance you would select fabric outer panels draped over a papier-mâché structure. Thankfully BMW stopped short of the recycled paper structure, but for some inexplicable reason its Gina Light Visionary Model used Lycra bodywork that would have offered nothing in the way of crash resistance – while anyone wielding a blade would have had a field day. It is not as if there was anything innovative going on underneath, as the Gina used the Z8's structure and running gear. Still, at least the car looked pretty neat – a saving grace that not all BMWs enjoy.

SPECIFICATION

ORIGIN	Germany
DEBUT	2008
ENGINE CAPACITY	4941cc (302cu in)
CONFIGURATION	Front-mounted V8
TRANSMISSION	Six-speed manual, rear-wheel drive
POWER	298kW (400bhp)
TOP SPEED	N/A
LENGTH	N/A
WIDTH	N/A

Left: *The key to the Gina was that fabric bodywork, which was capable of changing shape according to the speed of the car, providing variable aerodynamics.*

Even though Chris Bangle and his design team started on the Gina in 2001, the result would not be shown publicly until 2008.

The Z8's running gear was carried over unchanged, which meant there was a 298kW (400bhp) V8 up front – the same as the M5's.

One of the neater touches was the headlights; when not in use, the fabric around them could close up, like a blinking eye.

There were just four main elements to the bodywork: the combined bonnet (hood)/wings (fenders), the two sides and the rear deck.

CHEVROLET ASTRO III *(1961)*

If you are starting with a clean sheet of paper to design a car, the obvious thing to do is to get the wheel layout spot on, rather than somewhere close. Nobody suggested this to Chevrolet's designers, though, who clearly reckoned that, while a wheel at each corner is ideal for a car, putting two right next to each other was close enough; it was not. If you want to guarantee a lack of stability in a three-wheeler, you put the single wheel at the front – which is exactly where the Astro III's designers put the curious double wheel. Doh!

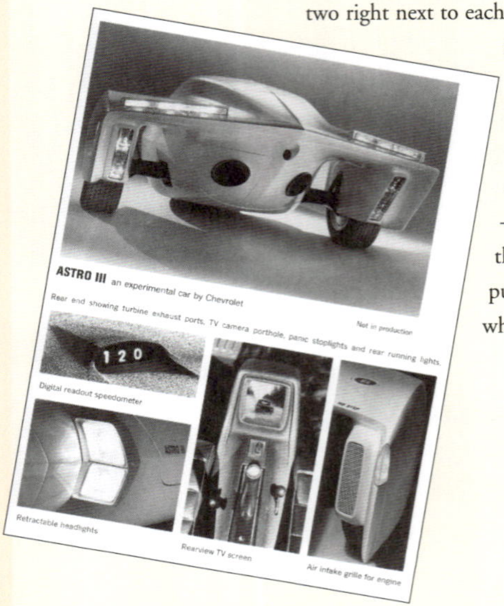

SPECIFICATION	
ORIGIN	USA
DEBUT	1961
ENGINE CAPACITY	N/A
CONFIGURATION	Rear-mounted gas turbine engine
TRANSMISSION	N/A
POWER	236kW (317bhp)
TOP SPEED	N/A
LENGTH	N/A
WIDTH	N/A

Left: ***The Astro III's canopy was power-assisted, while rear vision was provided by a television camera that fed images to an on-dash display.***

This was GM's lowest ever concept car, measuring less than one metre (three feet) high; occupants needed elevator seats to get in and out.

Power was provided by a Model 250-C18 gas turbine engine, produced by the Allison Division of General Motors.

The gas turbine engine was mounted at the rear, between the two rear wheels and hidden behind those pods.

It looks as if there is just one wheel in the nose of the Astro III, but there are actually two, next to each other.

CHRYSLER VOYAGER III *(1990)*

Concept-car designers have a habit of overcomplicating things, but Chrysler's team really excelled themselves here with an idea that was completely divorced from reality. A three-seater city car could be married with a separate rear pod, enabling the Voyager III to become an eight-seater people-carrier. In case this was not complex enough in itself, each part of the large vehicle featured its own powerplant, while there were also six wheels fitted – meaning three axles (complete with suspension), six tyres and six sets of brakes all to be maintained. If ever there was a set of ideas doomed to fail, it was to be found here.

SPECIFICATION

ORIGIN	USA
DEBUT	Detroit 1990
ENGINE CAPACITY	1.6 + 2.2 litres (98 + 134cu in)
CONFIGURATION	Front-mounted propane four-cylinder, rear-mounted petrol (gasoline) four-cylinder
TRANSMISSION	Four-wheel drive (when linked)
POWER	N/A
TOP SPEED	N/A
LENGTH	5042mm (199in)
WIDTH	N/A

Left: *Inspiration for the Voyager III cames from the James Bond movie* Thunderball, *in which Largo's yacht separates, with a smaller module sailing into the distance.*

The city car was fitted with a 1.6-litre (98cu in) propane-fuelled engine; the pod featured a 2.2-litre (134cu in) four-cylinder petrol (gasoline) unit.

The eight-seater Voyager III was claimed to be little longer than a regular Grand Voyager once it was up and running.

The driving force behind Voyager III was Bob Lutz, who had previously tried to get BMW, Opel, Ford and GM to take up the idea.

When the city car was mated to the rear pod, the rear wheels of the former were raised to prevent it becoming an eight-wheeler.

DODGE TOMAHAWK (2003)

It may look like a motorbike, but the Tomahawk actually featured four wheels – although the pairs were arranged so close together that it made little difference in terms of the stability available. Indeed, the wheels offered so little stability that this concept must be the most ridiculous in this whole book – even insane creations such as the Ford Nucleon and Nissan Pivo are positively rational alongside this. After all, how many people would be mad enough to strap themselves to a four-wheeler with the stability of a motorbike, but which was capable of around 483km/h (300mph), thanks to its 8.3-litre (505cu in) V10?

SPECIFICATION

ORIGIN	USA
DEBUT	Detroit 2003
ENGINE CAPACITY	8277cc (505cu in)
CONFIGURATION	Mid-mounted V10
TRANSMISSION	Two-speed manual, rear-wheel drive
POWER	373kW (500bhp)
TOP SPEED	483km/h (300mph)
LENGTH	2591mm (102in)
WIDTH	704mm (28in)

Left: *Dodge on the Tomahawk: 'This is a bold-faced slap against mediocrity; a scintillating example of what creative minds can do given the opportunity to run free.'*

Power was provided by the 8.3-litre (505cu in) V10 that usually resided in the nose of Dodge's Viper supercar; it generated a crazy 373kW (500bhp).

Those four wheels each measured 508mm (20in) across. The fronts were 102mm (four inches) wide; the rear 127mm (five inches) wide.

With a peak torque of 712Nm (525lbf ft), the V10 could push the Tomahawk to 97km/h (60mph) in just 2.5 seconds. There were just two gears, though.

The brakes were impressive, too, with a 508mm (20in) perimeter-mounted drilled rotor and four-pot callipers for each corner.

FORD GYRON (1961)

When it comes to unnecessary complication, few cars can beat this – just two wheels and a gyroscope system for stopping the whole thing from toppling over if the travelling speed dropped too low. Not only that, but the Gyron also featured a set of stabilizers that would automatically descend when the car was parked, to prevent it from landing on its side. Quite why Ford's designers did not just give the Gyron an extra pair of wheels – or even just the one wheel – was not disclosed. But, hey, this was the early 1960s, when the concept designer's maxim was 'the crazier the better'.

SPECIFICATION

ORIGIN	USA
DEBUT	Detroit 1961
ENGINE CAPACITY	Non-runner
CONFIGURATION	N/A
TRANSMISSION	N/A
POWER	N/A
TOP SPEED	N/A
LENGTH	N/A
WIDTH	N/A

Left: *Ford's designers believed that the day was coming when the car could drive itself, which is why there was an autopilot function that took care of everything.*

A screen ahead of the car's two occupants could display a clear view of the road ahead, regardless of lighting or weather conditions.

It was also possible to superimpose various pieces of information onto the screen, such as the Gyron's speed and its estimated time of arrival at a pre-set location.

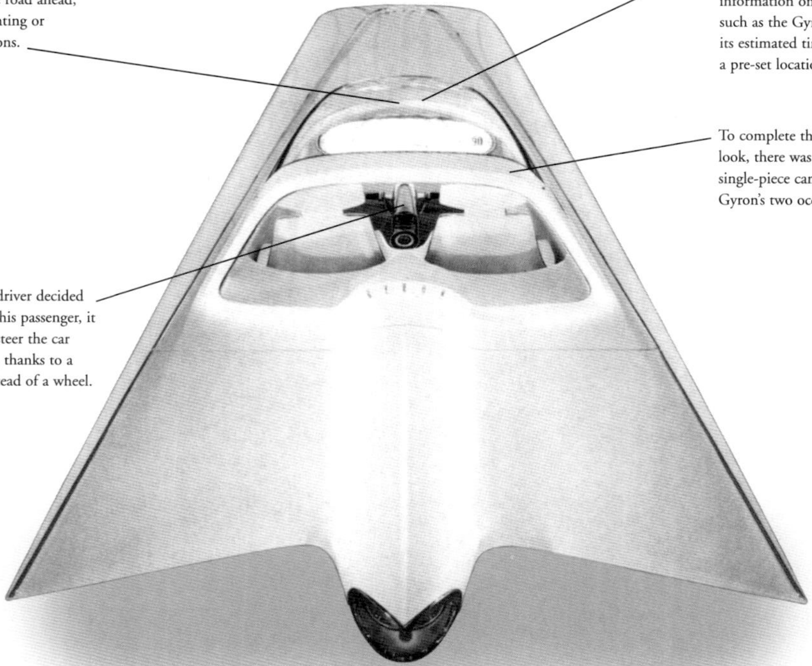

To complete the futuristic look, there was a rear-hinged single-piece canopy over the Gyron's two occupants.

Just in case the driver decided to hand over to his passenger, it was possible to steer the car from either seat, thanks to a steering dial instead of a wheel.

FORD SEATTLE-ITE XXI (1962)

Just for the appalling pun-laden name, Ford's design team should have been strung up, but at least this terrible creation never got beyond a 3/8 scale model. Unveiled at the 1962 Seattle World Fair (hence the name), the Seattle-ite 21's name also suggested a car for the twenty-first century – but we are still waiting for many of the proposed technologies to materialize. For example, while no specific motive power was listed for the concept, it was claimed to be capable of running on anything from petrol (gasoline) or electric to fuel cells or even nuclear power. Far out maybe, but at least this concept looked rather cool.

SPECIFICATION

ORIGIN	USA
DEBUT	Seattle 1962
ENGINE CAPACITY	Non-runner
CONFIGURATION	Front-mounted
TRANSMISSION	N/A
POWER	N/A
TOP SPEED	N/A
LENGTH	Scale model only
WIDTH	N/A

Left: *'Despite the generous proportions of the Seattle-ite, there was seating for just two – although it was very luxurious.*

No specific powerplant was proposed – instead there was a variety. Suggestions ranged from fuel cells driving electric motors to 'compact nuclear propulsion devices'.

The driver would not have any instruments; instead there would be a screen that displayed the car's functions, plus a navigation system.

Everything was computerized, with the driver able to read a display of the car's functions, as well as journey information.

All four of those front wheels were driven, while they also all steered – perhaps this was Ford's new way of reducing the effects of torque steer?

FORD LA GALAXIE *(1958)*

It looked shocking from every angle and packed proposals for technology that in some cases would not be available for decades – by which time the aesthetics would be massively dated. Still, Ford's La Galaxie gave its stylists something to do; this concept must have kept them amused for ages. Featuring such innovations as a reverse-rake rear window, twin boot (trunk) lids (one each side) and massive lighting units – those at the back were dubbed 'Vis-o-Rama' items – this certainly was not a bland concept. It was not even remotely feasible as a production car either, which is why very few aspects of it were ever available in anything on sale in Ford's showrooms.

SPECIFICATION

ORIGIN	USA
DEBUT	1958
ENGINE CAPACITY	Non-runner
CONFIGURATION	Probably front-mounted V8
TRANSMISSION	Automatic, rear-wheel drive
POWER	N/A
TOP SPEED	N/A
LENGTH	N/A
WIDTH	N/A

Left: *La Galaxie's steering wheel appeared to have been taken straight from a fighter aircraft. It incorporated the indicator and gearbox controls too.*

Many of the pieces of equipment proposed here would see production a long time hence; things such as the 'proximity warning apparatus'.

As was common at the time, there were flaps in the roof above each door; they lifted when the door was opened, to allow easier access.

There was seating for six, with the front chairs individually adjustable, to enable maximum comfort for the occupants.

Virtually everything was electrically operated, from the headrests and doors to the twin boot (trunk) lids and seats. They were controlled by switches ahead of the steering wheel.

FORD NUCLEON (1958)

It is perhaps a little unfair to include this automotive red herring here because Ford never took it beyond a 3/8 scale model – but just the fact that it was taken this far suggests its stylists and engineers were living on another planet in the 1950s. With World War II now a memory and the United States' prosperity growing every year, Ford embarked on a project that proposed nuclear power as a viable energy source for propelling road-going vehicles. Time has shown that such a notion is pure fantasy, but then isn't that what concept cars should sometimes be all about?

SPECIFICATION

ORIGIN	USA
DEBUT	1958
ENGINE CAPACITY	Non-runner
CONFIGURATION	Nuclear-powered
TRANSMISSION	N/A
POWER	N/A
TOP SPEED	N/A
LENGTH	Scale model only
WIDTH	N/A

Left: *Also unveiled by Ford in 1958 was the X-2000, which looked futuristic but was completely unworkable in pretty much every way.*

Most of the Nucleon's length was taken up by the atomic-powered energy source, which sat behind the forward-mounted cabin.

To optimize the aerodynamics, there were retractable bumpers front and rear – Ford did not disclose how they were activated.

To help reduce the nose line to a minimum, there were very slim horizontal headlights, a technical impossibility in 1958.

Unbelievably, there was a nuclear reactor sitting between those rear fins. It was suggested that there would be interchangeable units offered, with varying power outputs.

FORD FX-ATMOS (1954)

Few concept cars encapsulated the jet age better than Ford's FX-Atmos, which was unveiled to gasps of awe at the 1954 Chicago motor show. It seemed that, before long, everybody would be whizzing about at Mach 3 in a car that looked as if it had just arrived from Mars. Sadly it was not to be, though. There would be no huge glass canopies or afterburner-style exhaust pipes (at least not of this size), and the tail fins would generally be rather more discreet – not looking as if they had been appropriated from the nearest McDonnell-Douglas. Still, if you were a Jetsons wannabe, the FX-Atmos would have been perfect.

SPECIFICATION

ORIGIN	USA
DEBUT	Chicago 1954
ENGINE CAPACITY	Non-runner
CONFIGURATION	Probably mid-engined
TRANSMISSION	Probably automatic, rear-wheel drive
POWER	N/A
TOP SPEED	N/A
LENGTH	N/A
WIDTH	N/A

Left: *Something that you cannot appreciate with these black-and-white pictures is the car's patriotic colour scheme of red (bonnet/hood and rear wing/fender stripes), blue (rear deck) and white (everything else).*

There were twin antennae in the nose, one for each side. Just perfect for spearing any unfortunate pedestrians who got in the way.

A 'Roadarscope' scanned the road ahead, allowing the FX-Atmos to steer itself when the autopilot was set.

There was seating for three; the driver sat centrally up front, with each passenger to one side and slightly behind.

To keep the weight down while also simplifying the production process, the bodyshell was made of plastic – with all those details, metal would have been too costly.

GHIA ACTION *(1978)*

It is not clear whether it was the time that ran out or the money, but Ghia managed to design just half a car where the Action was concerned. The company got as far as the B-pillars, then called time on the project, having created the most amazing wedge-shaped profile that simply petered out just as it was getting going. Of course, Ghia put a positive spin on things, stating that it provided a 'basis for a research programme to pursue a study of its aerodynamic principles which could then be applied to the standard production family sedan'. Sounds fair enough – as long as the car in question offered just two seats, sat about a metre (three feet) high and offered styling that no self-respecting consumer was ever likely to venture anywhere near.

SPECIFICATION

ORIGIN	Italy
DEBUT	Turin 1978
ENGINE CAPACITY	3 litres (183cu in)
CONFIGURATION	Mid-mounted V8
TRANSMISSION	Manual, rear-wheel drive
POWER	N/A
TOP SPEED	N/A
LENGTH	N/A
WIDTH	N/A

Left: *By far the ugliest aspect of the Action was the flat rear end – it contained four exhaust pipes and numerous vents for the engine bay.*

To aid aerodynamics, the front wheels featured a flush design while the rear wheels were fully enclosed.

Forward visbility was aided by an incredibly deep wraparound windscreen – but the less said about rear visibility, the better …

Mounted out back was a Ford DFV 3-litre (183cu in) V8 – a nod towards the Action's proposed competition background.

Sitting just under a metre (three feet) high, the Action offered little in the way of practicality – although such a low height did do wonders for the aerodynamics.

IAD ALIEN (1986)

While the Alien was undoubtedly a break from the norm, the key technology that it previewed was doomed from the start – that of removable power packs. The idea was that the Alien owner could fit the engine that best suited the journey, but the entire back end of the car, complete with the suspension, had to be swapped at the same time – not exactly cheap or practical. Still, one area where the Alien succeeded spectacularly was in being the most jaw-dropping supercar ever devised – nobody could offer anything that came even close to those insect-like lines.

SPECIFICATION

ORIGIN	UK
DEBUT	Turin 1986
ENGINE CAPACITY	Variable
CONFIGURATION	Rear-mounted
TRANSMISSION	Rear-wheel drive
POWER	Variable
TOP SPEED	Variable
LENGTH	3690mm (145in)
WIDTH	1600mm (63in)

Left: ***The Alien was designed to look more amazing than the Lamborghini Countach; viewed from any angle, it succeeded in spectacular fashion.***

Instead of having doors that opened independently of each other, there was a canopy which, when raised, revealed the whole interior.

Safety was as important as performance, so there was a full roll cage in the Alien's structure, as well as side impact beams.

The rear-mounted engine pack was detachable, so that it could be unplugged and replaced with larger or smaller powerplants.

Handling and roadholding were optimized through various scoops, slats, ducts and spoilers at the front and rear, as well as down the sides.

MAZDA EX-005 *(1970)*

It is hard to argue that this is a concept *car* – the EX-005 was more of a concept golf cart. Well, at least that is what it looked like, even though Mazda was serious about this possibly offering a glimpse into the future of family transport. Proposed specifically as an urban commuter car, Mazda's EX-005 offered seating for four, but little in the way of comfort because those seats were of moulded plastic. The weather protection was also pitiful and, as far as crash safety was concerned, you can forget it. The power source was far-sighted, however, even if something of a dead end.

SPECIFICATION

ORIGIN	Japan
DEBUT	Tokyo 1970
ENGINE CAPACITY	200cc (12cu in)
CONFIGURATION	Mid-mounted Wankel with electric motor
TRANSMISSION	Automatic, central wheels driven
POWER	3kW (4bhp)
TOP SPEED	N/A
LENGTH	2500mm (98in) approx.
WIDTH	1500mm (59in) approx.

Left: ***The bodyshell was constructed from just three mouldings: the floorpan, the interior and the canopy, the last two of which were removable for access to the mechanicals.***

A constant-speed rotary engine provided energy for a battery, which in turn provided power for an electric motor. The whole thing sat in the middle of the car.

There was just one control in that amazingly spartan cabin – a centrally mounted joystick that took the place of the accelerator, brake pedal and steering wheel.

The EX-005 was pretty much symmetrical front to rear, as well as left to right, to keep manufacturing costs to a minimum.

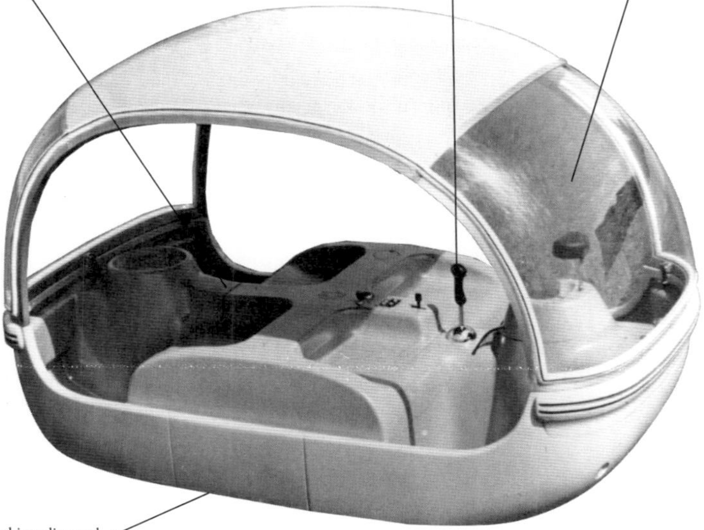

The wheels were arranged in a diamond formation, with the central pair driven. They moved at varying speeds for turning.

NISSAN PIVO (2005)

What possesses grown men and women to dispense with common sense altogether and come up with something as outlandish, as crazy, as utterly idiotic as this? So far removed from reality was the Pivo that it really did appear to have dropped in from another planet. Nissan's engineers took everyday items from the modern car and re-engineered them at what appeared to be maximum cost, to come up with a ludicrously overcomplex car that could never be economically viable. And to put the icing on the questionable cake, Nissan created a sequel to the Pivo two years later, predictably called the Pivo 2 and still packing far too much technology.

SPECIFICATION

ORIGIN	Japan
DEBUT	Tokyo 2005
ENGINE CAPACITY	Lithium-ion battery
CONFIGURATION	Front- plus rear-mounted electric motors
TRANSMISSION	Automatic, four-wheel drive
POWER	N/A
TOP SPEED	N/A
LENGTH	2700mm (106in)
WIDTH	1600mm (69in)

Left: *Instead of conventional hinges for the doors, they opened out and back on parallelogram hinges – yet more intricacy in an already complicated design.*

Instead of the Pivo being fitted with a reverse gear, the whole body pivoted through 360 degrees – a complex solution to a non-problem.

Freeing up space in the cabin and improving safety was a drive-by-wire system that dispensed with mechanical linkages.

Power was provided purely by electric motors. There was one for each axle, powered by a battery mounted in the centre of the car.

The driver could simply motion towards a sensor for the car to automatically activate various controls. Let's hope he or she did not sneeze at the wrong time …

PEUGEOT H2O (2002)

The 206 used to be one of Peugeot's smallest cars. Now think of your typical fire truck; most are the size of a small house, on account of the fact that they have to carry lots of people, water and all sorts of other gear such as ladders and cutting equipment. So how successful do you think it would be to marry the two together: a fire truck based on the Peugeot 206? If you needed to put out the fire in an ashtray you might be OK – but anything larger might conceivably need a vehicle with a bit more stature, n'est-ce pas? Perhaps that's why you have not seen many supermini-based fire trucks hanging around major conflagrations.

SPECIFICATION

ORIGIN	France
DEBUT	Paris 2002
ENGINE CAPACITY	Fuel cell
CONFIGURATION	Mid-mounted fuel stack
TRANSMISSION	Automatic, front-wheel drive
POWER	N/A
TOP SPEED	N/A
LENGTH	4294mm (169in)
WIDTH	1689mm (66in)

Left: *Peugeot justified the H2O concept by claiming that it was a reconnaissance vehicle for urban scenarios where larger vehicles could not gain access.*

It was utterly pointless, but the H2O looked good – and it was also fully functional with a water tank and (short) ladder.

Even though Peugeot is not renowned for its fire trucks, the H2O took the company's styling themes and used them to good effect.

The key technology on demonstration was the power source – a fuel cell. This powered electric motors that drove the front wheels.

Despite its functional nature, there were some sporty touches too. The key one was those 457mm (18in) polished alloy wheels.

PEUGEOT MOOVIE (2005)

Holy cow! When it comes to crazy concepts, the Moovie must take the cake, on account of it not containing a single useful or usable element within its whole design. It was created as a result of Peugeot's third annual design competition – this was chosen as the winner, even though there were masses of seriously great designs that had at least one foot in reality. Billed as an agile and environmentally friendly city car by its designer, André Costa, the Moovie was built as a full-scale model, but for some obscure reason Peugeot never committed to making the car available in its showrooms …

SPECIFICATION

ORIGIN	France
DEBUT	Frankfurt 2005
ENGINE CAPACITY	N/A
CONFIGURATION	N/A
TRANSMISSION	N/A
POWER	N/A
TOP SPEED	N/A
LENGTH	2330mm (92in)
WIDTH	1800m (71in)

Left: *The Moovie's two occupants sat on individual chairs behind what appeared to be an ironing board – that was the fascia.*

This concept won Peugeot's competition because of 'its original style expressing a clear allegiance with the marque' – well, it certainly wasn't derivative.

The interior was incredibly simple; two pods sat on top of the dash for the instrumentation, and, apart from the fascia and seats, that was about it.

There was a huge circular door on each side, which revolved for entry to the cabin. The door surrounds contained the driven wheels.

Perhaps the neatest touch was the front lighting, which was housed in the A-pillar. Above this were the rearview mirrors.

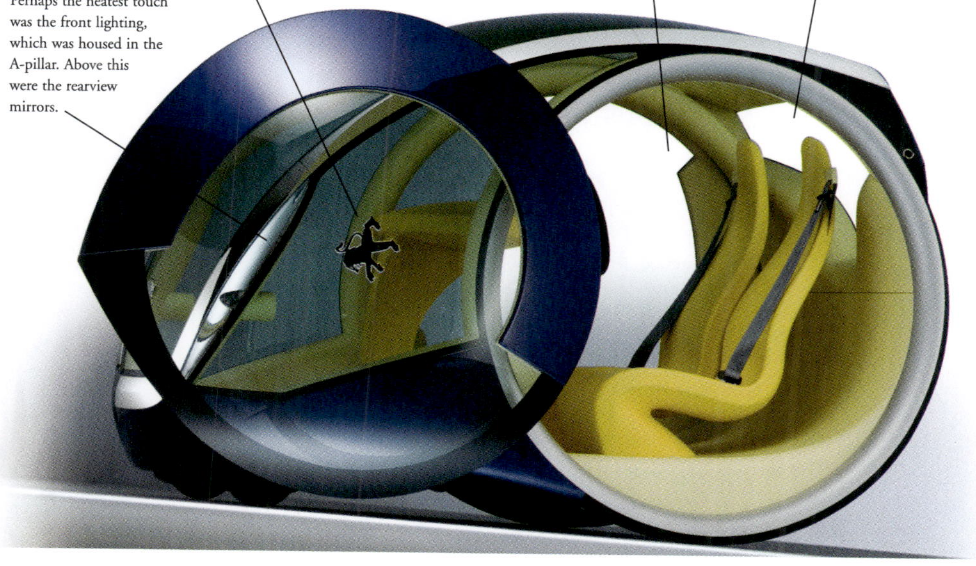

PININFARINA MODULO (1970)

A concept that is frequently held up as an all-time great, one that pushes the boundaries and that shows just why Pininfarina is the greatest design house ever … But why? Pretty much nothing included in the Modulo was usable in a production car, from the canopy to the enclosed wheels. Indeed, the Modulo's design introduces a mass of problems which need not be there in the first place, requiring intricate engineering at great cost. With modern technology it could just about be made driveable, but it is doubtful that was the case in 1970. Pininfarina may have created a motoring milestone, but it was about as relevant to the real world as a porcelain hammer.

SPECIFICATION

ORIGIN	Italy
DEBUT	Geneva 1970
ENGINE CAPACITY	4994cc (305cu in)
CONFIGURATION	Mid-mounted V12
TRANSMISSION	Five-speed manual, rear-wheel drive
POWER	410kW (550bhp)
TOP SPEED	N/A
LENGTH	4480mm (176in)
WIDTH	2040mm (80in)

Left: *The canopy slid forwards to give access to the two-seater cockpit. It was on rails, which had to go to the front of the car's nose when the canopy was fully open.*

Pininfarina created the Modulo without any consideration to practicality; this was a car built purely for form and nothing else.

The bodyshell was constructed from two halves, joined together around the car's waistline. This join was hidden by a moulding that incorporated the front and rear lights.

Those enclosed wheels seriously restricted the turning circle, and hence manoeuvrability, although they did help to improve the car's drag coefficient enormously.

Motive power was provided by Ferrari's fabulous 5-litre (305cu in) V12, taken from the 512 S racer and fitted in 410kW (550bhp) form.

RENAULT ZOOM (1992)

One of the requirements of any city car is that it must be cheap. Small and invariably offering little in the way of power or performance, city cars are usually attractive only because of their low price. And to sell a car cheaply it has to be made even more cheaply – which means reducing complexity to the minimum. Clearly nobody told Renault about these basics because, in conjunction with Matra, the French outfit produced perhaps the most complicated small car ever. The reason for that complexity: the two-seater Zoom featured a complex rear suspension that allowed its wheelbase to be varied according to conditions. Just what the world needed.

SPECIFICATION

ORIGIN	France
DEBUT	Paris 1992
ENGINE CAPACITY	Electric
CONFIGURATION	Front-mounted electric motor
TRANSMISSION	Automatic, front-wheel drive
POWER	25kW (34bhp)
TOP SPEED	120km/h (75mph)
LENGTH	2650mm (104in)
WIDTH	1520mm (60in)

Left: *Inside the Zoom, a bench seat offered space for two. Gadgetry was kept to a minimum, and the colours were funky to inject some youth appeal.*

To reduce weight the bodywork was made largely of composites. The car did not need to be painted; it was self-healing after a scrape.

In short-wheelbase mode, the Zoom was about a third of the size of a conventional small hatch and could be parked at right angles to the kerb.

The Zoom's wheelbase could be adjusted depending on driving conditions. At high speeds it would increase for a better ride – it could then be shortened for parking.

RENAULT RACOON (1993)

Take a helicopter, remove the rotor blades, then fit a set of wheels attached via the most complex suspension system imaginable – and you have the Renault Racoon. Answering a question that nobody in their right mind would ever ask, the Racoon was an amphibious off-roader that would have been thirsty (thanks to its twin-turbo three-litre V6 petrol engine), heavy (thanks to all the technology it packed) and also being not especially fast – it could not even crack the 160km/h (100mph) barrier. According to Renault, the Racoon's outlandish shape was defined 'by a powerful computer'. Seems as if it was not powerful enough.

SPECIFICATION

ORIGIN	France
DEBUT	Geneva 1993
ENGINE CAPACITY	2963cc (181cu in) twin-turbo
CONFIGURATION	Rear-mounted V6
TRANSMISSION	Six-speed manual, four-wheel drive
POWER	195kW (262bhp)
TOP SPEED	156km/h (97mph)
LENGTH	N/A
WIDTH	N/A

Left: ***Renault claimed that this was not a vehicle for rally raids or military use; it was clearly trying to tap into the nonexistent civilian amphibious market.***

The bodyshell was made of steel, which was mounted on a steel chassis. The result was a strong vehicle that was also heavy.

There were no windscreen wipers; instead the glass was chemically treated to disperse water. There was also an ultrasonic transmitter to disperse water.

For those who wanted to go off-roading at night, there was an infrared camera in the car's nose that transmitted pictures to an in-dash screen.

The ground clearance could be adjusted between 300mm (11.81in) and 500mm (19.69in), using the hydraulic suspension. There was 400mm (15.74in) of wheel travel.

TOYOTA POD (2001)

When the doors to the thirty-fifth Tokyo motor show opened in October 2001, Toyota had a frankly ridiculous 17 concept cars on display – as well as all of its regular production models. Most of these were vaguely normal, but that was not a term you could use to describe its Pod, a car that detected how its driver was feeling, and tried to interact. The Pod could detect its driver's pulse and perspiration rate, and Toyota claimed that it could then try to relax the driver – but all it could do was change the colour of its lighting and wag its 'tail' (an antenna on the back) – which was more likely to irritate the driver even further than placate them.

SPECIFICATION

ORIGIN	Japan
DEBUT	Tokyo 2001
ENGINE CAPACITY	1496cc (91cu in)
CONFIGURATION	Front-mounted four-cylinder
TRANSMISSION	Front-wheel drive
POWER	N/A
TOP SPEED	N/A
LENGTH	3930mm (155in)
WIDTH	1800mm (71in)

Left: *Each seat within the Pod was equipped with an individual display to allow passengers to enjoy their own music or video content, independent of the driver.*

The Pod's name was meant to evoke an image of a protective capsule that gently envelopes and protects family members.

The bodyshell was symmetrical from every view; the front, the rear and even the side. As a result, the car was pig ugly from every angle.

Even the Pod's interior was symmetrical, with seemingly identical controls and features for both driver and passengers.

The pod could exchange information with other vehicles to alert them of intentions such as overtaking; it could also thank them afterwards.

VENTURI ECLECTIC (2006)

If you are feeling down and need a laugh, glancing through some pictures of the Venturi Eclectic usually does the trick. This is the perfect antidote to the real world because this is a concept that is so far removed from reality that it is in another galaxy. The key thing about the Eclectic was that it was capable of producing its own power, thanks to its in-built solar panels and wind turbine. The problem was that it could not generate enough power to be truly usable; its range was limited and its top speed slow. Oh, and the looks were more than just a little bit challenging …

SPECIFICATION

ORIGIN	France
DEBUT	Paris 2006
ENGINE CAPACITY	Electric
CONFIGURATION	Electric motors
TRANSMISSION	Automatic
POWER	4kW (5bhp)
TOP SPEED	45km/h (28mph)
LENGTH	2783mm (110in)
WIDTH	1659mm (65in)

Left: *With a range of just 50km (31 miles) and a top speed of a mere 45km/h (28mph), the Eclectic was not in any danger of grabbing too many sales.*

There was seating for three, and because the Eclectic was classed as a quadricycle it could be driven in France by 16-year-olds.

The solar roof panels could generate just 72 watts – enough for a mere five kilometres' (three miles') worth of travel each day.

The wind turbine could generate up to 300 watts; that allowed 13km (eight miles) of travel a day. As long as it was windy, of course.

The double-wishbone suspension at each end was pure race car; sadly that is where the similarities ended. Very abruptly.

VENTURI ASTROLAB (2006)

As if one madly impractical concept was not enough to unveil at the 2006 Paris motor show, Venturi excelled itself by introducing something even crazier alongside the Eclectic shown on the previous pages. The Astrolab was effectively an even more extreme version of the Eclectic (who would have thought such a thing possible?). It was even more focused on harnessing solar energy, while dispensing with useful stuff such as carrying people. OK, so that last bit is not quite true – there was really space for two, but that was only on the basis that they did not want any creature comforts such as room to breathe or protection from the elements.

SPECIFICATION

ORIGIN	France
DEBUT	Paris 2006
ENGINE CAPACITY	Electric
CONFIGURATION	Electric motors
TRANSMISSION	Automatic
POWER	16kW (21bhp)
TOP SPEED	120km/h (75mph)
LENGTH	3800mm (150in)
WIDTH	1840mm (72in)

Left: *With 3.6 square metres (39 square feet) of solar panels on the bodywork, up to 600 watts could be generated – enough for 18km (11 miles) of travel each day.*

The batteries could also be topped up using a mains outlet; from exhausted to full, the process would take five hours.

All those solar cells led to a very flat-topped concept, which caused problems in itself – such as how to get into the two-seater cabin.

The key to the Astrolab's ultralight weight was its high-tech construction; the structure was alloy, while all panelling was carbon-fibre.

With a kerb weight of just 280kg (617lb), much of which was the battery pack, the Astrolab could hit a heady 120km/h (75mph).

ERRORS OF JUDGEMENT

The concepts in this chapter fall into two categories: those which should have gone into production, and those which should not have even reached the drawing board – never mind made it as far as working prototypes.

In the former category, the manufacturer in question invariably offered impossibly dull products in its showrooms, while trotting out great concepts that illustrated all too well what its designers were truly capable of. For example, while Cadillac churned out one angular box after another, its concept team was coming up with jaw-dropping creations like the Voyage and Solitaire. As Kia filled its showrooms with tedious machinery like the Shuma and Clarus, it's designers were dreaming up stunners like the KCV-III.

Then there were the cars which should never have been dreamed up, never mind created in three dimensions. Invariably ugly, these are the concepts which left the world a poorer place – and usually decimated potential customers' perceptions of what a brand could offer.

Left: *As Dodge lurched from one crisis to another, it found a solution in the Demon – but had no money to develop it.*

ALFA ROMEO KAMAL (2003)

You are responsible for some of the greatest driver's cars ever, even if they have the durability of rice paper. Your cars are also renowned for their brilliant styling, encompassing some of the sportiest styling cues around. So what do you do? You unveil an SUV, just because everyone else is doing it. Talk about watering down your brand values. Ah, you say, but Porsche did it, too, and its Cayenne was a success – so why not Alfa? The obvious answer to which is that Porsche is a German company, so it did the job properly. But Alfa Romeo, as an Italian company, would have got partway through, then run out of money as well as interest, creating another lame duck.

SPECIFICATION

ORIGIN	Italy
DEBUT	Geneva 2003
ENGINE CAPACITY	3179cc (194cu in)
CONFIGURATION	Front-mounted V6
TRANSMISSION	Six-speed semi-auto, four-wheel drive
POWER	186kW (250bhp)
TOP SPEED	217km/h (135mph)
LENGTH	4350mm (171in)
WIDTH	1860mm (73in)

Left: *The Kamal took its name from the Sanskrit for 'red' – even though the car featured gold paintwork. In Arabic the word means 'perfection'.*

A decent turbodiesel engine is essential for any compact 4x4 to succeed; that did not stop Alfa fitting the Kamal with a thirsty 3.2-litre (194cu in) petrol (gasoline) V6, though.

Bizarrely, its maker claimed that the 'Kamal reminds us of Alfa Romeo's glorious traditions in the sportscar sector'. Hmm. And how might that be?

Safety was a key attribute, with ESP and anti-lock brakes fitted. The centre of gravity was also lowered, to improve stability.

Even though an SUV can never be truly sporty, the Kamal would at least have injected some style into the segment.

AUDI SPYDER (1991)

The Spyder concept was a car that Audi should have made. Beautiful, a technological *tour de force* and fast as well as agile, thanks to its aluminium construction, this sportscar could have created its own market segment if only Audi had the confidence to put it into production – even if it had been in limited numbers. Safe, green, fast and stylish, the Spyder featured a super-strong yet light construction, roof-mounted solar panels to keep the battery topped up and performance galore from its 2.8-litre (169cu in) V6 powerplant. This was perhaps the biggest missed opportunity ever, as far as the performance car enthusiast was concerned.

SPECIFICATION

ORIGIN	Germany
DEBUT	Frankfurt 1991
ENGINE CAPACITY	2771cc (169cu in)
CONFIGURATION	Mid-mounted V6
TRANSMISSION	Five-speed manual, four-wheel drive
POWER	130kW (174bhp)
TOP SPEED	250km/h (155mph)
LENGTH	4215mm (166in)
WIDTH	1768mm (70in)

Left: ***It was the Spyder that kicked off Audi's fascination with aluminium construction; as well as a tubular alloy chassis, there were aluminium panels.***

Although the Spyder looks like a fixed-head coupé, its roof can actually be removed and stowed above the engine bay cover.

That lightweight construction kept the Spyder's kerb weight down to just 1100kg (2425lb), allowing a 0–100km/h (0–62mph) time of under six seconds.

Although there was just 130kW (174bhp) on tap, to transmit this as effectively as possible there was Audi's famed quattro four-wheel drive transmission.

Practicality was an important element; there was ample luggage capacity for the two occupants the Spyder could carry.

BENTLEY PROJECT HUNAUDIÈRES (1999)

You would be hard-pressed to call Bentley's offerings boring. Predictable or staid maybe – but definitely not boring. Perhaps the company is happy for things to be this way. After all, if it were not, the Crewe outfit would surely have put this into production – the Project Hunaudières. When the car was unveiled, Bentley and Lamborghini had just become part of the Volkswagen/Audi Group, and this was the parent company's way of showing the world what it could do. Bentley had never built a mid-engined car before, however, while Lamborghini was famous for it. Bugatti was also about to embark on a project to build the most ambitious supercar yet (the Veyron), so the Hunaudières remained nothing more than a concept.

SPECIFICATION

ORIGIN	UK
DEBUT	Geneva 1999
ENGINE CAPACITY	8004cc (488cu in)
CONFIGURATION	Mid-mounted V16
TRANSMISSION	Five-speed manual, four-wheel drive
POWER	465kW (623bhp)
TOP SPEED	In excess of 320km/h (200mph)
LENGTH	4432mm (174in)
WIDTH	1985mm (78in)

Left: *The Hunaudières took its name from the famous high-speed straight at Le Mans – the circuit where the presitigious Bentley brand built its following.*

To keep weight down, the bodyshell was made of aluminium and carbon-fibre, the latter also guaranteeing strength.

Predictably, the interior was superbly made, with Nubuck and Connolly leather, finished in green and tan.

The interior was littered with alloy details, as was the exterior; the spoilers and bumpers were solid aluminium.

There was a wire mesh grille, to maintain a family resemblance. It was cut down, though, to fit in with the ultra-low bonnet (hood) line.

BERTONE GENESIS (1988)

If you need proof of just how contrived the Genesis was, here is what Bertone had to say about it: 'high performance + spectacularity = pleasure/diversion'. Does that make sense to you? No? Well, the statement made as much sense as the car – which is none at all. Here was a people-carrier with a Lamborghini Countach V12 sitting in the middle – just what you need for cutting-edge packaging, low running costs and easy maintenance. Bertone reckoned that such a car would be feasible in time, as reliability improved – proving just how out of touch with reality this once-great design house had become.

SPECIFICATION

ORIGIN	Italy
DEBUT	Turin 1988
ENGINE CAPACITY	5167cc (315cu in)
CONFIGURATION	Mid-mounted V12
TRANSMISSION	Three-speed auto
POWER	339kW (455bhp)
TOP SPEED	N/A
LENGTH	4470mm (176in)
WIDTH	2057mm (81in)

Left: *There were huge gullwing doors for front-seat passengers and a conventional sliding door (but only on the offside) for rear-seat passengers.*

The interior was cossetting, but there were just five seats on offer – not very impressive for a genre designed for carrying lots of people.

The front passenger seat was able to swivel through 180 degrees, so that it faced the rear seats.

Although the Genesis was meant to be a sporty MPV, it was fitted with a three-speed automatic gearbox, which offered poor performance.

An all-glass tailgate, below which was a huge body-coloured bumper, allowed access to the luggage space.

CADILLAC VOYAGE (1988)

You could hardly call it a thing of beauty, but there is no denying the Voyage had presence, and it looked truly stunning in a rather offbeat kind of way. The flush glasshouse, heavily tapered nose and faired-in wheels gave the Voyage a genuinely futuristic look – yet at the time the company was busy churning out boxy saloons (sedans) such as its Eldorado, Seville, Fleetwood and Brougham. All these were a million miles away from the adventure and excitement suggested by the Voyage, which was a study in aerodynamics and high-tech equipment. What a shame it remained a mere study – this is just what Cadillac needed to get people into showrooms.

SPECIFICATION

ORIGIN	USA
DEBUT	New York 1988
ENGINE CAPACITY	4472cc (273cu in)
CONFIGURATION	Front-mounted V8
TRANSMISSION	Four-speed auto, rear-wheel drive
POWER	205kW (275bhp)
TOP SPEED	290km/h (180mph)
LENGTH	5400mm (213in)
WIDTH	1976mm (78in)

Left: *The Voyage's aerodynamic bodyshell was designed for maximum efficiency, as well as optimum stability at high speeds.*

Inside the Voyage was a cellular telephone that came complete with a hands-free feature.

The front spats turned with the wheels; the design helped to cut drag, but it nonetheless limited the available turning circle.

Instead of handles to upset the car's aerodynamics, remote controls were used to lock and unlock each door.

To help cut drag further, there were no externally mounted rearview mirrors; instead there were TV cameras relaying images to an on-dash screen.

CHEVROLET BEL AIR (2002)

When the Bel Air came out from under wraps at the 2002 Detroit motor show, Wayne Cherry, GM's vice president of design, claimed that this was 'not just another convertible'. But that is exactly what it was. Where were the flair and style of the mid-1950s original Bel Air? If there were any carried-over design cues, they were so watered down as to be barely recognizable. Indeed, trading in on the cachet of the classic Bel Air with this lame 21st-century concept was nothing less than a travesty – which must be one of the key reasons why Chevrolet did not take the car any closer to production. And we can all be grateful for that.

SPECIFICATION

ORIGIN	USA
DEBUT	Detroit 2002
ENGINE CAPACITY	3464cc (211cu in)
CONFIGURATION	Front-mounted five-cylinder
TRANSMISSION	Four-speed auto, rear-wheel drive
POWER	235kW (315bhp)
TOP SPEED	N/A
LENGTH	4852mm (191in)
WIDTH	1819mm (72in)

Left: *The basic architecture of the Bel Air's dashboard was vaguely reminiscent of the 1955–57 Tri-Chevys – but you had to look hard to catch the resemblance.*

In the nose was GM's Vortec 3.5-litre (211cu in) Vortec engine, driving the rear wheels via a four-speed automatic transmission.

The alloy wheels looked good, but again they did not reference the original car. They were polished alloy 457 x 203mm (18x 8in) items.

The rear light flipped up to provide access to the fuel tank filler – just as in the original Bel Air. But little else was inspired by the 1950s car.

The nose was perhaps the Bel Air's most disappointing aspect; it was bland and featured very little to connect it with its predecessor.

CHRYSLER ATLANTIC *(1995)*

The Atlantic may have been unashamedly retro, but that should not have stopped Chrysler from putting into production one of the most sensational concept cars ever designed. Sure, some of the proportions were slightly awkward, but there was nothing there that could not have been ironed out in the transition to production car. The brief was to come up with a concept that blended modern technology with the best elements of glamorous coachbuilt 1930s tourers; Bob Hubbach was the man responsible for the result. And you thought Giorgetto Giugiaro was a genius – but he never came up with anything that looked as sensational as this.

SPECIFICATION

ORIGIN	USA
DEBUT	Detroit 1995
ENGINE CAPACITY	4 litres (244cu in)
CONFIGURATION	Front-mounted eight-cylinder
TRANSMISSION	Four-speed auto, rear-wheel drive
POWER	268kW (360bhp)
TOP SPEED	N/A
LENGTH	5067mm (199in)
WIDTH	1925mm (76in)

Left: *Although there was a straight-eight engine under that V-shaped bonnet (hood), it was merely a pair of 2-litre (122cu in) Neon powerplants joined together.*

A four-speed automatic gearbox transmitted 268kW (360bhp) to the rear, but the Atlantic was not very fast because the gear ratios were never set up properly.

Inside there was lashings of leather, but no wood. Instead, to bring the car up to date, there was plenty of carbon-fibre detailing.

You would be hard-pressed to find a straight line anywhere within this design – it was a mass of curves that looked like something from another planet.

The ground clearance was far too great, but those 559mm (22in) wheels raised the ride height well beyond what it should have been.

CHRYSLER ME412 (2004)

It is perhaps a little unfair to include the ME412 here, as Chrysler may well have put it into limited production if it had not been so short of cash. But better product planning would have enabled the company to make some money rather than squander billions on cars that nobody wanted. Sure, the ME412 could only ever have been a niche product – but at least it is one that people would have actually aspired to, thanks to those fabulous razor-sharp lines, the massively powerful 12-cylinder engine and no doubt a price tag that would have made the car rather more affordable than comparable rivals.

SPECIFICATION

ORIGIN	USA
DEBUT	Detroit 2004
ENGINE CAPACITY	6000cc (366cu in)
CONFIGURATION	Mid-mounted V12
TRANSMISSION	Seven-speed auto, rear-wheel drive
POWER	634kW (850bhp)
TOP SPEED	400km/h (248mph)
LENGTH	4542mm (179in)
WIDTH	1999mm (79in)

Left: *Naturally there was space for just two inside, but there was plenty of luxury, with leather-trimmed carbon-fibre seat and equipment galore.*

The brakes were as impressive as the engine, with 381mm (15in) ventilated carbon ceramic ventilated discs with six-piston callipers.

For the ultimate in stiffness and lightness, there was a carbon-fibre bodyshell on a carbon-fibre and aluminium honeycomb tub.

The ME412's alloy wheels were equally impressive; 483 x 254mm (19 x 10in) items were at the front, while those at the rear measured 508 x 318mm (20 x 12½ in).

The rear spoiler was computer-controlled, to provide the best balance between downforce and minimal drag, at all speeds.

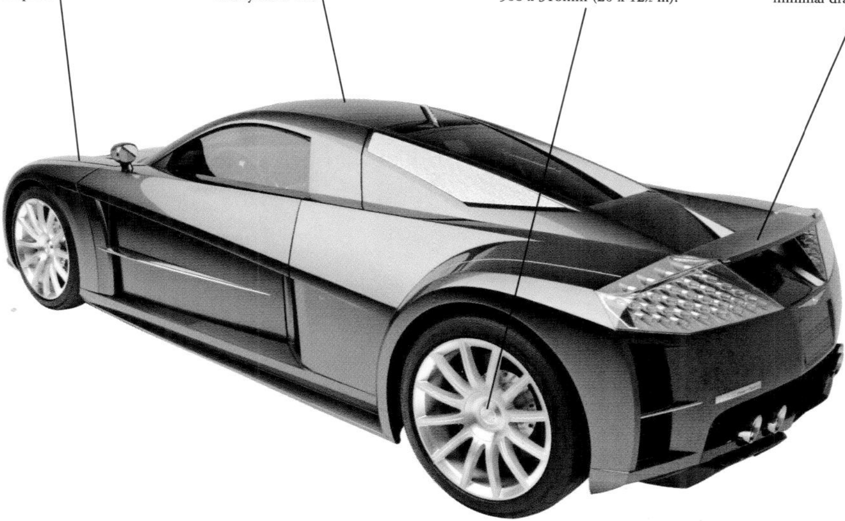

CITROËN ACTIVA (1988)

In the 1930s the Traction Avant arrived; this lasted until the 1950s when the DS made its debut. When the DS died the equally futuristic CX went on sale. But by the time this was killed off Citroën's range was getting rather stale – yet it need not have been this way. The French company was still capable of coming up with seriously far-reaching designs – it had just lost the will to put them into production. The Activa was proof of this, with its futuristic design and cutting-edge tech, but few of this concept's features featured on Citroën's production cars. Then the company did it all again just two years later, with the Activa 2 …

SPECIFICATION

ORIGIN	France
DEBUT	Paris 1988
ENGINE CAPACITY	3000cc (183cu in)
CONFIGURATION	Front-mounted V6
TRANSMISSION	Four-speed auto, four-wheel drive
POWER	149kW (200bhp)
TOP SPEED	N/A
LENGTH	4750mm (187in)
WIDTH	1900mm (75in)

Left: *There was masses of high-tech kit, with drive-by-wire featuring heavily. This replaced linkages with wires, potentiometers and sensors, opening up the cabin.*

As was typical for a Citroën, there were lots of high-pressure hydraulics, controlling the suspension and other major functions.

Citroën threw eveything it had at the Activa, with a 3-litre (183cu in) V6 engine, four-wheel drive, four-wheel steering and an automatic gearbox.

For the time, the amount of computer control was amazing; the Activa featured an active-ride suspension system for example.

The exterior design was incredibly stylish – and efficient, too, with a drag factor of just 0.25. Glass featured very heavily above the wasitline.

CITROËN GT *(2008)*

Citroën may have been rediscovering the art of good car design (if not construction) around the time that the GT was born, but none of its showroom offerings had anything like the drama of this amazing concept. Whereas most cars featured in computer games were based on real models, this one happened the other way around; an amazing hypercar was featured in Gran Turismo 5 and Citroën just had to build it. While the company produced the GT only as a concept, Citroën spoke of producing six road-going examples at around US$2 million apiece. As this book went to press, there was no sign, though …

SPECIFICATION

ORIGIN	France
DEBUT	Paris 2008
ENGINE CAPACITY	Fuel cell
CONFIGURATION	Mid-mounted fuel cell
TRANSMISSION	N/A
POWER	582kW (780bhp)
TOP SPEED	In excess of 320km/h (200mph)
LENGTH	4960mm (195in)
WIDTH	2080mm (82in)

Left: *Everywhere you looked there was visual drama, from the beetle-wing doors and rear diffusers to the wraparound glasshouse …*

A fuel cell generated electricity, which was fed to a motor on each of the four wheels. Citroën claimed a 582kW (780bhp) power output.

Thanks to a construction largely of carbon-fibre, the GT tipped the scales at just 1400kg (3086lb) – guaranteeing electrifying performance.

5. No wonder those wheels looked dramatic, as they measured 533mm (21in) across – 127mm (five inches) more than most supercar wheels.

To match the high-tech exterior looks, the cabin was also cutting-edge, with a head-up display and lots of copper for the trim.

DAEWOO MIRAE *(1999)*

Oh, dear; if only they had known. When the folks at Daewoo wrote the blurb for the Mirae, they confidently predicted that it 'showcases much of the thinking, design and technical innovation which Daewoo will deliver to the car buyer of 2010'. Little did they know that, by then, Daewoo would be a footnote in automotive history, as would GM Daewoo which succeeded it – and almost GM too. Still, at least they tried – and if the company had built anything with the style and technology that the Mirae offered, perhaps Daewoo would still be around now.

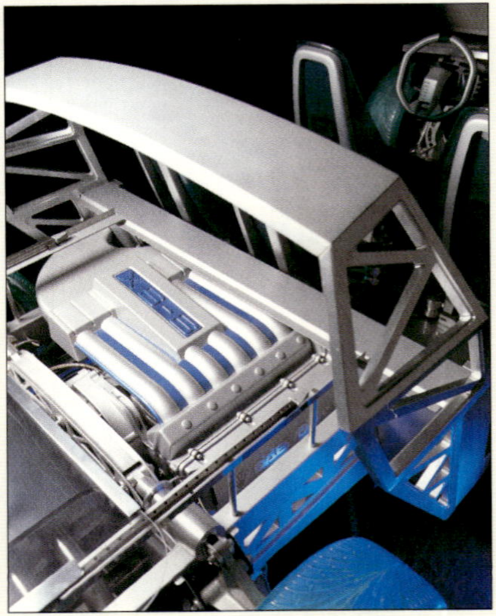

SPECIFICATION

ORIGIN	Korea
DEBUT	Seoul 1999
ENGINE CAPACITY	2492cc (152cu in)
CONFIGURATION	Front-mounted V6
TRANSMISSION	Six-speed auto, front-wheel drive
POWER	127kW (170bhp)
TOP SPEED	N/A
LENGTH	4160mm (164in)
WIDTH	1850mm (73in)

Left: *The key to the Mirae was practicality with performance – it had to offer a healthy dose of both, with plenty of style too.*

The drive-by-wire systems did away with mechanical linkages to free up cabin space and improve crash safety.
Daewoo attempted to dispense with a conventional-opening bonnet (hood), so a stronger, safer structure could be produced.
Key functions were controlled via digital cameras instead of buttons; the driver merely motioned for things to happen, and they did. Supposedly.
There were no door handles; entry was by a smart card instead. This increased security, while also helping the aerodynamics.

DAEWOO MYA *(1996)*

Daewoo had a habit of producing concept cars that put its production models in the shade. They were not always brilliantly proportioned and the build quality was not always there – but when it came to showing just how lame its own production cars were Daewoo often had things all sewn up. The Mya was a perfect example; looking like a cross between Ford's Puma and the McLaren F1 (thanks to those beetle-wing doors), it was neat and would have made the perfect budget sportster. But no. Instead, Daewoo decided to persist with the utterly dire Lanos and Espero. Good move.

SPECIFICATION

ORIGIN	Korea
DEBUT	Birmingham 1996
ENGINE CAPACITY	2 litres (122cu in)
CONFIGURATION	Front-mounted four-cylinder
TRANSMISSION	Five-speed manual, front-wheel drive
POWER	97kW (130bhp)
TOP SPEED	N/A
LENGTH	4280mm (169in)
WIDTH	1700mm (70in)

Left: *In true concept-car fashion, the Mya's doors featured a complex and costly hinge mechanism, which opened the doors upwards and outwards.*

Power was provided by Daewoo's in-house 2-litre (122cu in) engine, driving the front wheels via a five-speed manual gearbox.

The Mya was claimed to be a 2+2, but in reality the back seats were good for shopping bags only. Plenty of room in the front, though.

With those narrow headlights, sleek coupé styling and neat details, the Mya showed that Daewoo had some design skills – but did not use them often enough.

The wheel and tyre combination was sportier than the usual Daewoo fare; at each corner there were 457mm (18in) alloys with 225/40 ZR tyres.

DODGE DEMON (2007)

When Mazda introduced its MX-5 in 1989, it took the sportscar market by storm. Nearly two decades on, when Dodge unveiled its Demon concept, Mazda still had the affordable two-seater roadster market pretty much to itself – there was clearly room in the market for another contender or two. That was something that had not passed Dodge by, but the timing of this brilliant sportster's debut was all wrong. When the car was being developed, car sales were easy to come by, thanks to easy credit. Then a global recession struck, Dodge's parent company Chrysler went bust and the Demon was no more. It could have been a contender …

SPECIFICATION

ORIGIN	USA
DEBUT	Geneva 2007
ENGINE CAPACITY	2.4 litres (146cu in)
CONFIGURATION	Front-mounted four-cylinder
TRANSMISSION	Six-speed manual, rear-wheel drive
POWER	128kW (172bhp)
TOP SPEED	N/A
LENGTH	3974mm (156in)
WIDTH	1736mm (68in)

Left: *The Demon's black-and-alloy interior was a masterpiece because it was simple and understated, but well equipped and very neatly designed.*

In true sportscar fashion, there was a decently powerful engine in the nose, with the power being transmitted to the rear wheels.

No top speed was announced, but with a kerb weight of just 1179kg (2600lb) and a handy 128kW (172bhp) on tap, performance would not have been lacking.

At each corner there was a brushed aluminium 483mm (19in) alloy wheel, specially designed and with a neat five twin-spoke design.

The Demon was billed as a 'roadster with attitude', thanks to that aggressive treatment, flared arches and bodywork creases. In short, it looked great.

DODGE ZEO (2008)

If the Demon had been a victim of unfortunate timing, the ZEO was even more so. Nobody could have foreseen the financial storm that was to break loose just a few short months after the Zeo's unveiling – a meltdown that guaranteed Dodge would never find the money it needed to build such a far-sighted car. Indeed, the whole automotive landscape would be changed by this episode, with the Chrysler Group hit especially hard. In reality, the company probably would not have been able to afford to develop it anyway; if it had done so, the ZEO would have been one hell of a car.

SPECIFICATION

ORIGIN	USA
DEBUT	Detroit 2008
ENGINE CAPACITY	Electric
CONFIGURATION	N/A
TRANSMISSION	Rear-wheel drive
POWER	203kW (272bhp)
TOP SPEED	210km/h (130mph)
LENGTH	4390mm (173in)
WIDTH	1944mm (76in)

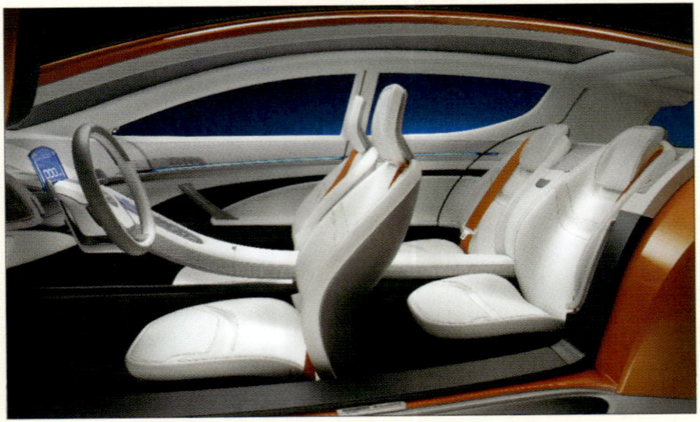

Left: *There was a 2+2 seating configuration; a central console ran the length of the ZEO's interior, splitting it into two right to left.*

This was a sportscar for tree huggers; despite running on electricity, the ZEO could cover the 0–97km/h (0–60mph) sprint in just 5.7 seconds.

The lithium-ion batteries gave a 400km (250-mile) range, but they had to be recharged by plugging the car into an electricity supply.

'ZEO' stood for 'Zero Emissions Operation', on account of the car's motive power coming from a single electric motor.

Those wheels were a bit over the top, as they measured 584mm (23in) across. The tyres were 40-profile at each corner.

JAGUAR F-TYPE *(2000)*

Shamelessly copying the XK180, when it was unveiled the F-Type showed that Jaguar was capable of designing stunning-looking sportscars. But instead the Ford offshoot insisted on serving up the X-Type, S-Type and XJ, all of which looked as if they had driven straight out of the 1960s. Yes, it was derivative and it definitely displayed a lack of imagination as a result, but why produce a concept as gorgeous as this, then refuse to build it? With production of its XJ and XK in tiny numbers, and nobody wanting its X-Type and S-Type saloons (sedans), the company clearly desperately needed a product that somebody would actually want to buy. Apparently this was obvious to everyone except the management at Jaguar.

SPECIFICATION

ORIGIN	UK
DEBUT	Detroit 2000
ENGINE CAPACITY	2967cc (181cu in)
CONFIGURATION	Front-mounted V6
TRANSMISSION	Five-speed auto, rear-wheel drive
POWER	179kW (240bhp)
TOP SPEED	N/A
LENGTH	4115mm (162in)
WIDTH	1732mm (68in)

Left: *Using all of the classic Jaguar styling cues, the F-Type was just as curvaceous and inviting as the E-Type that had been launched nearly 40 years before.*

It looked as if a massive hugely powerful engine should have been installed, but there was just a 3-litre (181cu in) V6, rated at 179kW (240bhp).

The show car featured no form of weather protection – engineering a full roof would have spoiled the car's gorgeous lines.

The interior was as simple as the exterior, but there was plenty of aluminium trim, machined from solid billets, then polished to perfection.

The oval grille and faired-in headlights were inspired by the first E-Types. The same applied to the muscular haunches over the rear wheels.

KIA KCV-III (2003)

When Kia unveiled the KCV-III in 2003, the most exciting car in its product range was the Sorento 4x4. If you were really unlucky and lived in the wrong part of the world, you could even buy a Hyundai Atoz-alike, called the Visto. So to dangle a sportscar such as the KCV-III in front of prospective customers and continue churning out cars that were as dull as ditchwater seemed rather unfair to say the least. Where were 508mm (20in) alloys and sweeping curves to be found in Kia showrooms? Nowhere – but this concept showed that at least Kia knew they existed. There had certainly been no evidence of this before.

SPECIFICATION

ORIGIN	Korea
DEBUT	Frankfurt 2003
ENGINE CAPACITY	2 litres (122cu in)
CONFIGURATION	Front-mounted four-cylinder
TRANSMISSION	Five-speed manual, front-wheel drive
POWER	108kW (145bhp)
TOP SPEED	N/A
LENGTH	4100mm (161in)
WIDTH	1820mm (72in)

Left: ***Compact convertibles were expected to pack a folding hardtop by 2003; a soft-top would not do. That's why the KCV-III had a retractable hardtop.***

The hardtop was a neat two-piece affair, which essentially consisted of a glass roof panel and a glass rear window, attached via a folding frame.

The interior was trimmed in light leather; this was officially a 2+2, but those in the back needed to be amputees to fit.

Those looks were striking rather than attractive; the plunging waistline and stubby nose looked very odd, as did the nose with its tiny grille.

Proposed technology included mobile telematics, an integrated radar system and cutting-edge entertainment. The car was built by Heuliez.

KIA SIDEWINDER *(2006)*

If you were asked to name a car maker at the performance end of the market, one that offered exciting designs, shattering speed and the most amazing dynamics this side of a Lotus Elise, the chances are you would not volunteer Kia. So a car as focused as this wearing Kia badges may not compute, but as the Sidewinder was penned in the Korean company's American Design Centre there was not much chance of it appearing under any other car maker's flag. The Sidewinder was designed specifically for drifting – a sport that cannot have seen too many Kias taking part. Still, truth is often stranger than fiction; maybe we will yet see something like the Sidewinder become a Kia production reality.

SPECIFICATION

ORIGIN	Korea
DEBUT	Los Angeles 2006
ENGINE CAPACITY	N/A
CONFIGURATION	Natural gas, turbine
TRANSMISSION	Rear-wheel drive
POWER	N/A
TOP SPEED	N/A
LENGTH	N/A
WIDTH	N/A

Left: *Kia chose drifting as the theme for the Sidewinder because Los Angeles was the scene of the first officially sanctioned North American drifting event.*

Power came from a compressed natural gas turbine, which supplied electricity to a series of in-wheel high-torque electric motors.

The man behind the proposal was Marc Mainville, who penned the Sidewinder as part of the Los Angeles Auto Show design contest.

There was room on board for just two people – although in reality just the one seat was needed while drifting.

The Sidewinder was never intended to be more than a design proposal; Kia did not even build a model of the car.

LAGONDA SUV (2009)

Many decades ago, Lagonda built sporting cars for the discerning gentleman. It was then swallowed up by Aston Martin, which eventually turned it into a mere model – and a seriously unreliable wedge-shaped one at that. For some reason, even though the Lagonda badge had nothing but negative connotations for many, Aston Martin decided to resurrect the brand – on a bloated and disfigured SUV. Unsurprisingly, the car was lambasted by all who saw it, with the result that the project went no further. Conveniently, the global recession was blamed for a lack of available investment funds, which just goes to prove that every cloud has a silver lining.

SPECIFICATION

ORIGIN	UK
DEBUT	Geneva 2009
ENGINE CAPACITY	5935cc (362cu in)
CONFIGURATION	Front-mounted V12
TRANSMISSION	Four-wheel drive
POWER	N/A
TOP SPEED	N/A
LENGTH	5199mm (205in)
WIDTH	N/A

Left: *The purpose behind the Lagonda SUV was to give Aston Martin access to profitable emerging markets such as Russia, China and South America.*

Despite its massive dimensions, the SUV could accommodate just four people, each of whom was given their own sculpted seat.

While the concept featured a conventional petrol engine, Aston Martin talked of petrol (gasoline)/electric hybrids, as well as diesel powertrains.

Although the Mercedes GL provided a platform for the SUV, motive power came from Aston Martin's own V12 engine.

Specially made for the concept were the 559mm (22in) alloy wheels, which featured ultra-thin rims with low-profile tyres.

LAMBORGHINI ESTOQUE (2009)

If you were asked to name the most dramatic supercars of all time, it is almost inevitable that there would be a few Lamborghinis on your list. After all, what can top a Countach, never mind a Murciélago SV? When it comes to jaw-dropping design language, Lamborghini has long had things all sewn up. So what a shame that the Italian outfit got things so badly wrong with this four-door saloon (sedan) proposal, assuming that its supercar design cues would survive the transition from one configuration to another. It is almost a blessing that the Estoque was unveiled in the midst of global financial turmoil, which resulted in the car being canned. Thank heavens.

SPECIFICATION

ORIGIN	Italy
DEBUT	Geneva 2009
ENGINE CAPACITY	N/A
CONFIGURATION	Front-mounted engine
TRANSMISSION	Four-wheel drive
POWER	N/A
TOP SPEED	N/A
LENGTH	5150mm (203in)
WIDTH	1990mm (78in)

Left: *One of the few elements of the Estoque that looked really good was the new design of five-spoke 559mm (22in) alloy wheels.*

The Estoque was a non-runner, but it could have featured V10 or turbocharged V8 petrol (gasoline) engines, or even hybrid or turbodiesel power.

The Estoque took its name from a sword used by a matador in a bull fight; most of Lamborghini's model names are bull-related.

Lamborghini had built four-seater (and 2+2) cars before, but it had never actually put a four-door car into production.

The engine was located in the nose, which meant that there was a raft of cooling slots and ducts to feed air into the radiators, as well as the brakes.

LAMBORGHINI CALA (1995)

There are some who believe that no Lamborghini is complete unless it has a dozen cylinders – but not everybody can afford such a machine. As a result, more affordable models are always in demand by car makers, who need to churn out as many vehicles as possible each year, to enjoy some economies of scale. So what a shame that Lamborghini created this fabulous entry-level car in the mid-1990s, then failed to capitalize on it. Fast, distinctive and more affordable than a Diablo, this could have been just the car to take the fight to Ferrari – which it did not manage until the twenty-first century, thanks to its lack of conviction.

SPECIFICATION

ORIGIN	Italy
DEBUT	Geneva 1995
ENGINE CAPACITY	3900cc (238cu in)
CONFIGURATION	Mid-mounted V10
TRANSMISSION	Six-speed manual, rear-wheel drive
POWER	298kW (400bhp)
TOP SPEED	291km/h (181mph)
LENGTH	4390mm (173in)
WIDTH	1900mm (75in)

Left: *Powering the Cala was a 3.9-litre (238cu in) V10 engine, mounted in the middle of the car and driving the rear wheels only.*

The Cala was a fully functioning prototype, designed and built by Italian styling house Italdesign. It looked sensational from every angle.

The Cala featured a targa configuration, as the roof panel was removable. This panel also featured glass inserts to lighten the cabin.

The exterior design was seriously dramatic, with scoops, slats and spoilers all over the place. Every one of them was there for a reason.

Lamborghini had made several V8-powered cars before, but none captured the imagination in the way that its V12 models did. Maybe that is why the Cala never made production.

LANCIA FULVIA *(2003)*

Lancia had been withering on the vine for years when it unveiled its Fulvia concept in 2003. Plundering classic models had proved successful for several marques over the previous decade, so Lancia figured that the strategy was worth a go. How could it fail, when the Fulvia went down a storm with everyone who saw it? The assumption was made that it looked too good for it to not go into production. With strong demand guaranteed, Lancia then did the obvious thing – it pulled the plug on the project. Well, it had to; its dealers would not know how to cope with a model that anybody actually wanted to buy.

Left: ***The Fulvia's interior looked just as great as its exterior, with plenty of brown leather, pale wood and brushed alloy details.***

SPECIFICATION

ORIGIN	Italy
DEBUT	Frankfurt 2003
ENGINE CAPACITY	1747cc (107cu in)
CONFIGURATION	Front-mounted four-cylinder
TRANSMISSION	Five-speed manual, front-wheel drive
POWER	103kW (138bhp)
TOP SPEED	225km/h (140mph)
LENGTH	N/A
WIDTH	N/A

The concept was built around Fiat Barchetta running gear; production cars would use the new Fiat Grande Punto as its basis.

The Barchetta basis meant that there was front-wheel drive – not ideal for an enthusiast's car, but it meant lower production costs.

The Fulvia concept took most of its styling cues – interior and exterior – from the original 1960s production car of the same name.

The bodywork was made of aluminium to keep weight down; there was a toughened Perspex roof to lighten up the cabin.

LAND ROVER RANGE STORMER (2004)

What a wasted opportunity. After unveiling the star of the 2004 Detroit motor show, Land Rover then watered down its Range Stormer concept to the point where it was pretty much unrecognizable. Sure, the Range Rover Sport that resulted was a highly covetable machine – but compared with the original concept it was as desirable as chicken pox. Despite the disappointments that would follow, the Range Stormer was highly significant because it was Land Rover's first ever concept car. The company was clearly a quick learner; like so many others it had worked out how to build up hopes with a great-looking concept, only to disappoint when the production car was unveiled.

SPECIFICATION

ORIGIN	UK
DEBUT	Detroit 2004
ENGINE CAPACITY	N/A, supercharged
CONFIGURATION	Front-mounted V8
TRANSMISSION	Six-speed sequential, four-wheel drive
POWER	N/A
TOP SPEED	N/A
LENGTH	N/A
WIDTH	N/A

Left: ***The cabin was fitted with four individual seats, with natural materials dominating; leather, oak and aluminium featured heavily.***

A stack of Range Rover design cues were incorporated, such as the clamshell bonnet (hood), floating roof and the bonnet's castellated corners.

Terrain Response allowed the driver to tell the car the terrain that it was tackling, so that the electronic control systems could keep the car moving.

The doors were complex; the top opened up and forwards, while the lower part dropped to provide a step into the cabin.

Emphasizing the Range Stormer's sporty nature, there were massive 559mm (22in) alloy wheels fitted front and rear.

MASERATI KUBANG *(2003)*

Is there a motoring genre more distantly placed from the racing car than the SUV? It is hard to think of one, so when Maserati came up with this proposal for a plush 4x4 there was no shortage of people questioning the sanity (as well as the parentage) of those in charge. Of course, Maserati would have been quick to point to Porsche, which had corrupted its own brand values with the Cayenne – but Porsche was a much bigger company that could afford to take the risk. Thankfully those at Maserati realized that the company was too small to risk putting a 4x4 into production, so the project was quietly canned.

SPECIFICATION

ORIGIN	Italy
DEBUT	Detroit 2003
ENGINE CAPACITY	4244cc (259cu in)
CONFIGURATION	Front-mounted V8
TRANSMISSION	Six-speed semi-auto, four-wheel drive
POWER	291kW (390bhp)
TOP SPEED	254km/h (158mph)
LENGTH	4984mm (196in)
WIDTH	1942mm (76in)

Left: ***Neither Maserati nor Italdesign liked to think of the Kubang as an SUV; it was a cross between a conventional 4x4 and a sporting estate (station wagon).***

To optimize the dynamics, there was an almost perfect weight distribution, while the centre of gravity was 100mm (four inches) lower than the typical SUV's.

The cabin was luxurious and practical too. Five seats were standard, or there was a four-seat option – while a third row could also be added.

This was a monster of a 4x4; even though it was nearly five metres (16½ft) long, it could still manage 0–100km/h (0–62mph) in just 5.5 seconds.

As is traditional for Maseratis, the Kubang is named after a wind – in this case, one that emanates from Java.

MASERATI BURAN *(2000)*

Maserati has one of the richest histories of any car maker anywhere; it is a brand that is covered in racing glory, has offered some of the most beautiful cars ever built and has provided some of the most impressive engineering in the history of the car. So why did it put its name to this large hatch-profile saloon (sedan) that looked as if it should have been wearing Daewoo badges? Take the trident off the nose and this car could easily have come from Korea or China, such was its lack of flair. It may have packed a 276kW (370bhp) 3.2-litre (195cu in) engine and been billed as an ultra-high performance luxury saloon, but you turned up at the Ritz in one of these you would probably be sent packing.

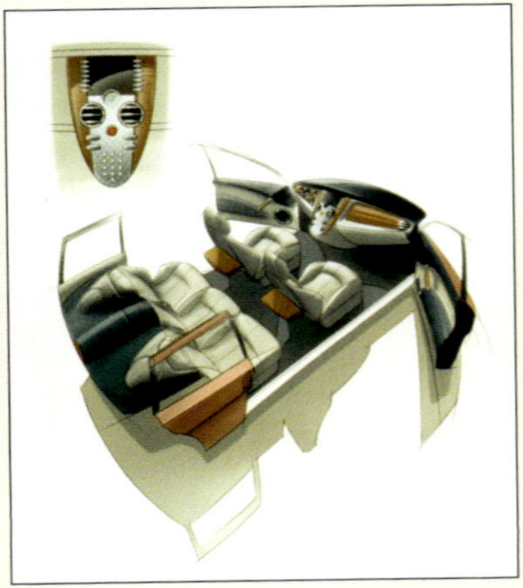

SPECIFICATION

ORIGIN	Italy
DEBUT	Geneva 2000
ENGINE CAPACITY	3.2 litres (195cu in) turbocharged
CONFIGURATION	Front-mounted V8
TRANSMISSION	Four-wheel drive
POWER	276kW (370bhp)
TOP SPEED	N/A
LENGTH	4983mm (196in)
WIDTH	1950mm (77in)

Left: ***The rear row of seats in the Buran featured three individual chairs, each of which could be adjusted separately, or folded flat to create a worktop.***

Captains of industry like to be chauffeured about in large saloons (sedans) – this hatchback reeks of practicality where it should reek of class.

As if the hatchback profile was not enough, those rear doors slid backwards and forwards – just like on an MPV. Not very classy.

The Buran's interior was inspired by the grand tourers of the 1930s, with an art deco feel and plenty of matt suede.

The saving grace of the Buran was its bulk; at almost five metres (16½ft) long, it matched a standard-wheelbase Mercedes S-Class.

MAZDA KABURA *(2006)*

During the first decade of the twenty-first century, Mazda showed a series of radical concepts that gave a taste of what its production cars might look like over the coming years. Least radical was the Kabura, which Mazda claimed could go into production with relatively few changes; had it done so, the car would have been guaranteed to be an instant sell-out. But instead Mazda got cold feet and the project was shelved, with the company sticking to its more conventional 3 and 6 models instead. Good lookers they may have been, but neither was a patch on the Kabura.

SPECIFICATION

ORIGIN	Japan
DEBUT	Detroit 2006
ENGINE CAPACITY	2 litres (122cu in)
CONFIGURATION	Front-mounted four-cylinder
TRANSMISSION	Six-speed manual, rear-wheel drive
POWER	N/A
TOP SPEED	N/A
LENGTH	4050mm (159in)
WIDTH	1780mm (70in)

Left: *The Kabura took its name from the Japanese word* kabura-ya*, which is used for the first arrow fired in battle, signifying the beginning of a conflict.*

Instead of the more conventional 2+2 seating layout for a sportscar, Mazda offered a more useful 3+1 set-up.

The windscreen went right up into the roof, while there was also a glass panel in the bonnet (hood), to show off the powerplant.

There were 483mm (19in) wheels at the front, while those at the back were 25mm (one inch) larger. Tyres were 245/35 items all round.

Instead of a rotary engine, Mazda fitted a conventional piston unit that displaced 2 litres (122cu in); it was fitted in the nose.

MITSUBISHI CONCEPT RA (2008)

Sometimes you look at a concept and your first thought is that it just must be built. Sadly, more often than not, the concepts which reach production are those that least deserve to – but it was the other way around here. The Ra was so fabulous in every way that it seemed almost imperative that Mitsubishi put it into showrooms – but it failed to do so, preferring instead to peddle its Colt and Lancer, both of which were OK, but far from exciting. The Ra, by contrast, would have injected some real fire into the brand – combined with Evo mechanicals it would have slain all rivals.

SPECIFICATION	
ORIGIN	Japan
DEBUT	Detroit 2008
ENGINE CAPACITY	2179cc (133cu in) turbocharged
CONFIGURATION	Front-mounted diesel four-cylinder
TRANSMISSION	Six-speed semi-auto, four-wheel drive
POWER	150kW (201bhp)
TOP SPEED	N/A
LENGTH	4445mm (175in)
WIDTH	1895mm (75in)

Left: *The interior fused retro design with modern references, using natural materials throughout such as leather and aluminium. The roof was made of glass.*

The engine visible through the bonnet (hood) looked great, but this feature would have stopped the Ra passing strict pedestrian safety laws.

Unusual for a sportscar – and especially a Japanese one launched in the United States – was the turbodiesel engine, giving torque with economy.

The key to the Ra's fabulous looks was the cab-forward stance, even though the powerplant sat in the nose.

Using much of the technology usually seen in the Evo, the Ra also featured four-wheel drive and a twin-clutch transmission.

NISSAN FORIA (2005)

Sometimes you do not have to try too hard to come up with a truly beautiful shape. Take the Nissan Foria, for example. Understated, classy, distinctive and modern, this four-door coupé had everything Nissan needed for a premium family car that could compete with the best. But just as Nissan unveiled the Foria, it was pretty much abandoning the family saloon (sedan) market, opting instead to build one SUV after another. If only it had seen this car through to production, it would have offered a real alternative to the dull mid-sized saloons that proliferated; instead, we got the Qashqai and X-Trail, which were very poor substitutes in style terms.

SPECIFICATION

ORIGIN	Japan
DEBUT	Tokyo 2005
ENGINE CAPACITY	N/A
CONFIGURATION	Front-mounted
TRANSMISSION	Rear-wheel drive
POWER	N/A
TOP SPEED	N/A
LENGTH	4350mm (171in)
WIDTH	1695mm (67in)

Left: *Nissan did not cite a power source for the Foria, merely saying that the engine was 'mid-size'. It drove the rear wheels via a paddle-shift gearbox.*

There were no extraneous details on the bodywork. Everything was there for a purpose, and the result was seriously stylish.

Highlighting the fact that this was a four-door coupé, the roof line sloped sharply towards the rear of the Foria.

The interior worked just as well as the exterior, with a retro feel courtesy of brown and magnolia leather trim, and alloy detailing.

Many of the exterior details were made of alloy, such as the windscreen surround and the air vents at the back of the front wings (fenders).

PEUGEOT PROXIMA (1986)

In 1986 the fastest, most glamorous Peugeot you could buy was a turbocharged 205 with four-wheel drive. OK, so the 205 T16 was a rallying icon, but it was still a world away from the Proxima, as well as the Oxia, that succeeded it, and the Quasar which pre-dated it by two years. All three were outlandish mid-engined supercars that promised excitement that Peugeot simply could not deliver when it came to showroom-ready cars. Instead, Peugeot's factories churned out the 309, 504 and 604. All worthy cars maybe, but where was the excitement that Peugeot's designers and engineers proved they could offer, given just half a chance?

SPECIFICATION

ORIGIN	France
DEBUT	Paris 1986
ENGINE CAPACITY	2850cc (174cu in) twin-turbo
CONFIGURATION	Mid-mounted V6
TRANSMISSION	Five-speed manual, four-wheel drive
POWER	447kW (600bhp)
TOP SPEED	N/A
LENGTH	4420mm (174in)
WIDTH	2060mm (81in)

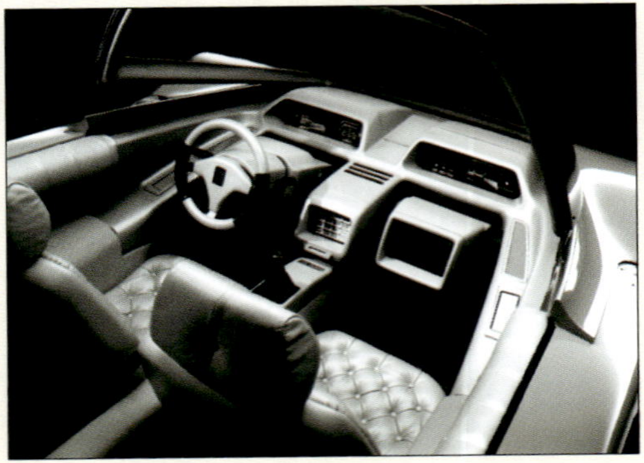

Left: ***The Proxima's cabin had space for two in comfort, and another two behind who enjoyed very little space. Everything was trimmed in bright red. Nice ...***

To keep weight down while maintaining crash resistance, the bodywork was made of carbon-fibre; the canopy was polycarbonate.

There was a massive 447kW (600bhp) on tap, thanks to a twin-turbo 2.85-litre (174cu in) V6. Each turbo had its own air-to-water intercooler.

Very advanced for its time was a computer that controlled the multipoint fuel injection, ignition timing and idle speed.

The transmission was also controlled by electronics. A lever on the centre console activated microswitches that operated the clutch.

PLYMOUTH PRONTO SPYDER *(1998)*

Plymouth was part of the Chrysler Group, which has struggled ever since its heyday in the 1960s. Constantly on the verge of bankruptcy, Chrysler has produced one lemon after another – but it need not have been like that. Just a quick look at the Pronto Spyder shows that its designers were capable of truly great work – there is not an angle from which this car does not look sensational. OK, so two-seater convertibles will never sell in the same numbers as family saloons (sedans), but Plymouth could have done a lot worse than to offer the Pronto Spyder in its showrooms as a halo product.

SPECIFICATION

ORIGIN	USA
DEBUT	Detroit 1998
ENGINE CAPACITY	2429cc (148cu in) supercharged
CONFIGURATION	Mid-mounted in-line four-cylinder
TRANSMISSION	Five-speed manual, rear-wheel drive
POWER	168kW (225bhp)
TOP SPEED	225km/h (140mph)
LENGTH	3926mm (155in)
WIDTH	1753mm (69in)

Left: *Plymouth's Pronto Spyder followed up a hatchback Pronto that had been shown in 1997. That was good, but nowhere in the same class as this.*

This could have been a great budget sportscar. With its 168kW (225bhp) 2.4-litre (148cu in) four-cylinder engine, strong performance was guaranteed.

This was almost called the 'Gator' because the Spyder's lines were reminiscent of an alligator about to strike – according to Plymouth.

The entire bodyshell was made from an advanced injection-moulded plastic, which allowed more intricate detailing than before.

Good dynamics were a given, thanks to the engine being fitted in the middle of the car and the Spyder's light weight.

PONTIAC SUNFIRE (1990)

While Pontiac churned out motoring horrors such as the Le Mans, 6000 LE and Bonneville, it was busy also creating fabulous concepts such as the Sunfire, which offered all of the aesthetic pizzazz that its production contemporaries lacked. This was not a one-off either; other greats included the Banshee, Stinger and Salsa – none of which got even close to production. Pontiac would go on to adopt the Sunfire name for its 1995 line of small cars, but that was not a model that offered anything like the style of this concept – which proved that the brand had the potential, but it just refused to share it with its customers.

SPECIFICATION

ORIGIN	USA
DEBUT	Detroit 1990
ENGINE CAPACITY	2400cc (146cu in) turbocharged
CONFIGURATION	Front-mounted in-line four
TRANSMISSION	Five-speed manual, front-wheel drive
POWER	142kW (190bhp)
TOP SPEED	N/A
LENGTH	4547mm (179in)
WIDTH	N/A

Left: *To keep the car's weight down while also maximizing stiffness and strength, the Sunfire's bodyshell was manufactured from carbon-fibre.*

Those really uncluttered lines were aided by a lack of door handles, in a bid to improve aerodynamics and keep the lines uncluttered.

There were four seats and four doors, the rear doors being hinged along their back edge. With no central pillar, entry and exit were easy.

Very much about efficiency, the Sunfire had a 142kW (190bhp) turbocharged 2.4-litre (146cu in) four-cylinder engine fitted.

Unusually, the headlights flipped up at the base of the windscreen; at the rear there were full-width tail-lights.

RENAULT WIND *(2004)*

Somebody at Renault must have been having a laugh when they suggested that the French company should name its new concept 'Wind' – or perhaps connotations of flatulence were what they wanted conjured up when the car was unveiled. Whatever the thinking behind the name, the Wind was one of those concepts that really should have made production. While the windscreen was too upright and some of the proportions were wrong, the basic concept was just right – a cheap sportscar designed to take on the Mazda MX-5. Sadly, Renault continued to churn out hatchbacks instead, letting another opportunity pass it by.

SPECIFICATION

ORIGIN	France
DEBUT	Geneva 2004
ENGINE CAPACITY	1998cc (122cu in)
CONFIGURATION	Front-mounted four-cylinder
TRANSMISSION	Six-speed manual
POWER	101kW (136bhp)
TOP SPEED	N/A
LENGTH	3870mm (152in)
WIDTH	1750mm (69in)

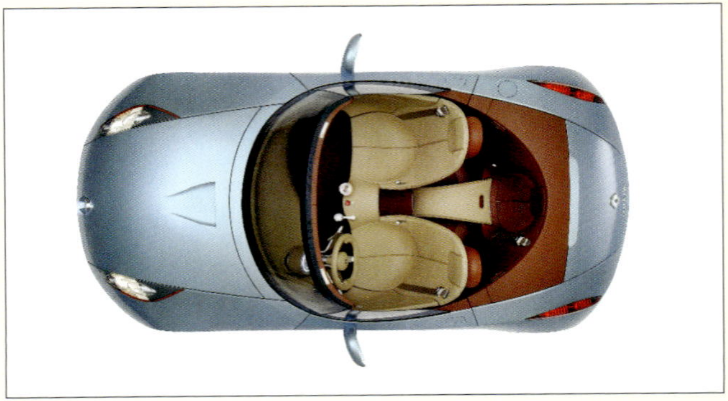

Left: *The Wind's cabin was very simple, but beautifully crafted. The seats were covered in tan leather, with the rest of the trim finished in a deep red.*

Unusually, the Wind was a three-seater. There were two seats up front and another squeezed between them and behind.

The six-speed gearbox featured automatic or sequential manual modes; ratios were changed using steering wheel-mounted paddle shifts.

The headlights swept partway up the front wings (fenders), just like those on Renault's Vel Satis and Talisman concepts – very stylish.

Strong performance was guaranteed, thanks to a kerb weight of just 850kg (1874lb); there was a useful 191Nm (141lbf ft) of torque and 101kW (136bhp).

RENAULT ZOE (2005)

Renault's first-generation Twingo had been a massive success throughout Europe, thanks to its cheeky looks, low price and brilliant cabin versatility. So when the Zoe was unveiled it was assumed that this was to be Twingo Mk2 – another great looker with a clever cabin and tiny exterior dimensions. Alas, it was not. Instead, this was a concept that would lead nowhere, while the real second-generation Twingo was just another small hatch that could have come from any mainstream motoring brand. The fact that the second take on the Twingo was an also-ran was regrettable – that Renault had teased us with this great concept first made it even more so.

SPECIFICATION

ORIGIN	France
DEBUT	Geneva 2005
ENGINE CAPACITY	1.2 litres (73cu in) turbocharged
CONFIGURATION	Front-mounted four-cylinder
TRANSMISSION	Clutchless manual, front-wheel drive
POWER	74kW (99bhp)
TOP SPEED	N/A
LENGTH	3450mm (136in)
WIDTH	1680mm (66in)

Left: *The Zoe's doors slid open electrically; above the front seat were glass panels that featured a sky-at-night design using LEDs.*

A clutchless manual five-speed gearbox was activated by paddle shifts on the steering wheel. Drive went to the front wheels.

The Zoe previewed an all-new turbocharged 1.2-litre (73cu in) petrol (gasoline) engine that Renault would use in its forthcoming superminis.

Up to three people could be accommodated, and there were three different configurations for the seats.

Most of the Zoe's lighting was taken care of by light-emitting diodes (LEDs); they were used for the headlights as well as the tail-lights.

SAAB AERO X *(2005)*

Perhaps the best word used to describe Saab's production cars is 'inoffensive'. Some might also say 'bland', but one adjective you certainly could not use is 'exciting'. Yet the Aero-X was exactly that – with its wraparound windscreen, which was part of an all-enveloping canopy, along with its pointed nose, the Aero-X was a real stunner. Even the wheels looked fantastic, based on the design of turbine blades – they gave the car the sort of presence that Saab's production cars lacked. Yet this Swedish company appeared incapable of moving on to inject any presence into its production cars – something which was proved yet again with the unveiling of an all-new 9-5 in 2009 … which looked just like the old one.

SPECIFICATION

ORIGIN	Sweden
DEBUT	Geneva 2005
ENGINE CAPACITY	2.8 litres (171cu in) twin-turbo
CONFIGURATION	Front-mounted bio-ethanol V6
TRANSMISSION	Seven-speed semi-auto, four-wheel drive
POWER	298kW (400bhp)
TOP SPEED	250km/h (155mph)
LENGTH	4657mm (183in)
WIDTH	1918mm (76in)

Left: *The Aero X's bodyshell was made of carbon-fibre, underneath which was adjustable suspension and four-wheel drive.*

That massive wraparound glass canopy used aircraft principles – it also offered a 180-degree field of vision.

All interior and lighting was by light-emitting diode (LED), for greater efficiency and reliability; this type of lighting is also much more compact.

The Aero X was a real performance machine with its 298kW (400bhp) twin-turbo V6, but it was clean, too, as it ran on bio-ethanol.

The Aero X's interior was as avant-garde as the exterior, with three-dimensional instrumentation and translucent displays. There was seating for just two.

SATURN CURVE (2004)

When the Curve was unveiled in 2004, Saturn did not have a great track record with its car styling. Indeed, the company was perhaps unique in offering a range of cars that were without exception somewhat aesthetically challenged – every model was a dog. So to see a really good-looking new model unveiled by this GM offshoot was a breath of fresh air. All that was needed was for the company to commit to building it. Sadly, this was not to be. Instead, Saturn continued churning out one ugly duckling after another – lemons such as the Ion, Relay and Vue, although at least the Sky offered a break from the tedium. But not for long …

SPECIFICATION

ORIGIN	USA
DEBUT	Detroit 2004
ENGINE CAPACITY	2200cc (134cu in) supercharged
CONFIGURATION	Front-mounted four-cylinder
TRANSMISSION	Five-speed manual, rear-wheel drive
POWER	172kW (230bhp)
TOP SPEED	N/A
LENGTH	3975mm (156in)
WIDTH	1811mm (71in)

Left: *Although the interior was relatively high-tech in its design, the dominant feature was a slab of light-coloured wood.*

The Curve was based on GM's new Kappa platform, which underpinned several of the company's smallest production cars.

As a result of the pillars hiding behind the glass, the roof appeared to be floating; all of the Curve's glazing was flush.

Although the Curve looked like a two-seater, there was actually seating for four – not that there was much space in the rear.

Those wheels were 508mm (20in) in diameter, while the brake discs measured a hefty 356mm (14in) across; plenty for this 2.2-litre (134cu in) car.

SEAT FORMULA *(1999)*

As the twentieth century became the twenty-first, worthy family cars were all that SEAT appeared capable of producing. Ibizas, Toledos and Alhambras were rolling off the VW offshoot's production lines, but here was a glimmer of hope – an affordable mid-engined sportster that looked sensational, was great to drive (the concept was a runner) and would lift the Spanish brand above the humdrum. But, no, in its infinite wisdom SEAT decided that it made more sense to churn out superminis and family hatches, denying enthusiasts the chance to get behind the wheel of something truly desirable from within its ranks.

SPECIFICATION

ORIGIN	Spain
DEBUT	Geneva 1999
ENGINE CAPACITY	2 litres (122cu in) turbocharged
CONFIGURATION	Mid-mounted in-line four
TRANSMISSION	Six-speed semi-auto, rear-wheel drive
POWER	186kW (250bhp)
TOP SPEED	240km/h (149mph)
LENGTH	3943mm (155in)
WIDTH	1758mm (69in)

Left: *Apart from the large SEAT badge on the grille, there were not many clues as to the origins of the Formula – but it was distinctive.*

Following the same back-to-basics theme as the Lotus Elise, SEAT's Formula put driving pleasure above absolutely everything else.

Those air vents in the rear wings (fenders) fed air into the engine bay, but there were still plenty of scoops and slats at the front of the car.

Ensuring strong performance was a 186kW (240bhp) 2-litre (122cu in) turbocharged engine, linked to a six-speed sequential manual gearbox.

The interior was simple, with no more than the bare minimum of trim. This restraint allowed the beautifully crafted aluminium tub to be shown off.

SUBARU B5-TPH (2005)

It would be fair to say that Subaru was not creating too many stylistic masterpieces when the B5-TPH was unveiled. What with its universally unloved Tribeca SUV, plus the Impreza hatch which replaced the previous saloon (sedan) and estate (station wagon), Subaru's design team appeared to have gone well and truly off the boil. Yet despite these disasters, Subaru was clearly capable of producing great-looking cars – it just seemed to be incapable of putting them into production. The B5-TPH was just such a car; it looked slick and was perfectly proportioned, yet Subaru did not use any of its styling themes for its production cars. Complete madness!

SPECIFICATION

ORIGIN	Japan
DEBUT	Tokyo 2005
ENGINE CAPACITY	2 litres (122cu in)
CONFIGURATION	Front-mounted flat-four plus electric motor
TRANSMISSION	Six-speed manual, four-wheel drive
POWER	194kW (260bhp)
TOP SPEED	N/A
LENGTH	N/A
WIDTH	N/A

Left: *Although Subaru claimed that this was a coupé, the B5-TPH was really a cross between a three-door hatchback and an estate (station wagon).*

The electric motor put out just 10kW (13bhp), but a very useful 149Nm (110lb ft) of torque, to liven things up in the acceleration stakes.

'TPH' stood for 'Turbo Parallel Hybrid'; this referred to the electric motor between the engine and transmission, designed to boost performance.

At the heart of the electric motor was a manganese lithium ion battery that could be charged to 95 per cent capacity in just five minutes.

As with most Subarus, four-wheel drive was fitted. There was also 200mm (7.87in) of ground clearance, so that the all-wheel drive could be used.

VAUXHALL VX LIGHTNING (2003)

If you were asked to come up with highlights from Vauxhall's first 100 years of car production, you would probably struggle to come up with anything more than sporty editions of humdrum family cars, such as the Chevette HS and Droop Snoot Firenza. So when the GM offshoot unveiled the VX Lightning, to celebrate its first centenary in business, things were looking rosy. The problem was that the Lightning did not signal the start of a Vauxhall design revolution; sure, the VX220 emerged soon after – but that was merely a much-watered down version of this concept. Vauxhall's range as a whole did not benefit, despite the fact that creativity was clearly there.

SPECIFICATION

ORIGIN	UK
DEBUT	2003
ENGINE CAPACITY	2171cc (133cu in) supercharged
CONFIGURATION	Front-mounted four-cylinder
TRANSMISSION	Six-speed manual, rear-wheel drive
POWER	179kW (240bhp)
TOP SPEED	N/A
LENGTH	4100mm (161in)
WIDTH	1908mm (75in)

Left: *It was GM's Kappa platform that enabled the Lightning to be built; this also sired the Pontiac Solstice, Opel GT and the Saturn Sky.*

Power came from GM's 2.2-litre (133cu in) four-cylinder Ecotec unit, tuned to give a healthy 179kW (240bhp) in supercharged form.

Thanks to setting the powerplant well back, it was possible to achieve a weight distribution that was almost 50:50 front to rear.

The sculpted seats looked fantastic; they were trimmed in black and red leather, with red hide used to finish off the dashboard.

Although it looked like the Lotus Elise–based VX220, the Lightning was very different, with an engine in the nose.

INDEX